THE PAWN

A Novel By

Gustavo "Goose" Alvarez

The Pawn
Copyright 2020

ISBN: 978-0-578-63579-8 (paperback)

All rights reserved.

DEDICATION

I dedicate this book in memory of *Mr. Leonard Kallen*. Your guidance was truly God's work.

FOREWORD

During 2015 and 2016 I spent 18 months at a medium security prison ("short time" by normal US standards). I was there as a free man – a researcher, studying penal labor by observing and working alongside prisoners in their mandatory labor assignments. Outsiders like me are uncommon in such facilities. Thanks to this rare access, I was able to observe firsthand the trying conditions that millions of incarcerated individuals are all too familiar with. Throughout the country, corrections budgets are tight while prisoner populations remain massive. Many facilities have responded by cutting costs and corners. In addition to requiring more and more incarcerated people to work, many have decreased the size of meals in the chow line, begun providing fewer meals on weekends, trimmed back educational and vocational programming, and introduced a list of fees for prisoners to pay for everything from electricity to emergency doctor visits. As I grew close to the captive laborers at my research site, it was evident that they badly needed the meager wages from their mandatory work assignments in order to get by.

At this particular prison, the most popular item that workers purchased with their earnings was by far ramen noodles from the commissary. To possess a "soup" was to possess valuable currency that could be used on the black market to buy things like additional food, necessary hygiene products, and an array of illicit services. As I contemplated what it was about ramen that gave it such power in the underground economy, I discovered an invaluable resource in the form of a cookbook called *Prison Ramen*. The book helped inspire me to write a research paper on ramen and informal currency behind bars. This is how I first got acquainted with Gustavo "Goose" Alvarez, one of the cookbook's authors. Through recipes and memorable stories, he and his collaborators pulled back the veil – at least briefly – on the carceral experience by highlighting the practical and symbolic importance of a seemingly simple packet of noodles.

Accounts from the inside such as those in *Prison Ramen* are key for those of us in the free world to truly comprehend the nature of the beast that is mass incarceration. As I continued researching prison life and labor from within, countless individuals that I met expressed their need to be *heard* in this way – to share their stories, whether through preaching or performing, mentoring or writing, or countless other outlets of expression. Some would succeed; many more would be halted by the same hurdles that helped direct them toward prison in the first place. Although Goose was not held at the institution where I did my work, he shares with these men a desire to impart his knowledge and experiences.

Goose's new book, *The Pawn*, represents only the latest in a rich and ongoing series of tales that he has to share. In it, he tells a story that was in many ways inspired by real struggles and sorrows, compromises and triumphs. Like a Westside Dostoyevsky, Alvarez translates some of his own troubling experiences and observations to the page through the lens of fiction, but the author's personal voice is never lost in the process. Nor does he shy away from gritty truths. To be sure, the book does not censor scenes of violence or strife. It is visceral but honest. *The Pawn* portrays the competing rewards and risks of life on the inside with nuance and respect. As the main character navigates the minefield of the prison yard, we are made privy to many of the hidden realities of mass incarceration. We see institutionalization take hold as bloodshed and racial politics become normalized for our protagonist, who must adapt quickly to survive the indignities and hostilities of confinement. Racialized gang structures often appear to be as rigid and demanding as the institution itself. Tribalism seems inescapable, though it often runs up against potential pathways to escaping this life.

Underlying it all, we get a view into an institution that systematically limits outlets for dignity and self-betterment while facilitating violence. With few trade schools or classroom opportunities available to develop marketable skills and hope for the future, those inside face pervasive drug use and may see recidivism as imminent. The prison described in *The Pawn* – like its real world counterparts throughout the country – exhibits what researchers call "criminogenic" effects. That is, rather than contributing to rehabilitation, it fosters an environment where helpful ties to family and loved ones on the outside become severed, stigmas are ascribed to the imprisoned that will continue to haunt them even after release, and feelings of anger and resentment are intensified. As a result, successfully reentering mainstream society seems more and more difficult, while opportunities to secure respect and economic stability through criminal endeavors may appear with greater consistency.

Years of research support what Goose demonstrates: Prisons are "treadmills." The incarcerated face intense pressures to conform to sometimes contradictory sets of rules and expectations amidst ever-shifting systems of control. Influences from all sides seek to strip them of their outside identities and rebuild them with new selves, better situated to fulfill the needs of those atop different hierarchies. Many recount how quickly one may feel carried away by these processes. Additionally, prisons are sometimes said to have "revolving doors." Of the half a million or so individuals returning home from captivity in any given year, some studies suggest that nearly three-quarters may come back into contact with the criminal justice system within just five years. This can be attributed to many different factors. Two important ones are the fact that rehabilitation and reentry programs have been scaled back across the board, and that the neighborhoods to which former prisoners return often remain just as stricken by hardship and limited opportunities as when they first entered the system.

These and other harsh realities of the contemporary prison remain purposefully concealed from the view of the general public. The millions who pass through such institutions each year are at risk of remaining "out of sight and out of mind." Yet, authors such as Goose do the rest of us an important service: They reveal that which is hidden. *The Pawn* illustrates contemptible conditions of confinement on U.S. soil without ever denying the actions, emotions, and compromises that have shaped the author's perspective. By reading this book, you amplify the voice of one who, like so many others, had been "disappeared" by the American legal system, but who may now be truly heard.

Dr. Michael Gibson-Light

ACKNOWLEDGMENTS

To my family, who have supported me through my life and have shown me what truly matters.

Kevin D. Kallen, thank you for never shying away from speaking the truth and always being available to offer your direct and incisive assessment of my writing and ideas. I am grateful for your guidance, friendship, and support with this project.

Jesse Alvarez, thank you for giving me the wise guidance necessary to get my views expressed most effectively in this project.

I would like to express my sincerest gratitude to *Dr. Michael Gibson-Light* of the University of Arizona School of Sociology for his ethnographic field work and research of US state prisons.

Finally, to my kids: *Destiny, Daisy, Giovanni,* and *Faith.* YOU are my reason. Love you above all else.

INTRODUCTION

Two years into my prison term I did what seemed the only sensible thing to do: I attacked and stabbed my mentor.

Within seconds I had successfully completed the hit—a direct order from a Mexican shot caller. Like an animal hunting for prey, I repeatedly stabbed a man in the neck and upper body as his energy bar diminished. On one hand, I had no clue what I was doing, yet on the other hand, I did it with the precision of a hired gun and the coolness of someone who had done this many times before.

With the first two strides, I walked slowly and purposefully. As I neared the end of the corridor, the speed of my gait increased, my heart fluttered, my pulse quickened, and my legs weakened. *Ten yards to go. Three strides.* I was there. I was out in the yard. By now my pace had increased to a jog. I scampered through the dirt field. With adrenaline pumping through my veins, I headed towards the outdoor restroom.

My roll dog, Spider, was sitting there on the toilet waiting on me. "Quickly, hand me the shank!" he yelled. As he flushed it, I made my way back towards the track and blended in with the joggers. I had done it. I had murdered one of the higher-ups. A shot caller if you will. Someone they said who was untouchable.

When the lockdown came, I flopped down on my bed in complete exhilaration at what I had accomplished. I was a young inmate doing hard time in a maximum security prison with little or nothing to show for it, but now my stock had gone up. Now my status would rise even higher and the level of respect that would now be bestowed upon me would ascend above anything that I had ever experienced in the past. I had arrived.

As my mind whirled upon all these thoughts, my insides turned, my stomach ached, my throat tightened, and before I knew it, I found myself clinging to the stainless steel toilet with my head buried deep within. I puked like there was no tomorrow. Tears streamed down my cheeks and the realization of what I had done set in. I had killed a special friend. The first person that tried to do something for me that in the long run would have benefited me. I had betrayed that. It was who I had become.

CHAPTER 1

My family and I lived right across the street from Inglewood High School. Most White people never saw this area unless they were going to a Lakers game.

As a twelve-year-old boy, I thought myself to be a bit of a tough individual. No one could influence me to do something I didn't want to do, or at least that's what I thought. Day by day I was changing and didn't even know it. I was being disarmed of the little common sense that I possessed at the time.

When I played outside, the older guys made it seem that it was cool to be them. When I turned on the TV, the advertising agencies made me believe that I needed those sneakers that my parents definitely couldn't afford. When the movie flipped back on, it was cool to be the bad guy or the good guy, as long as I had a gun. When I turned to my father, being a provider was his focus, so most of the time he wasn't there. I was getting the wrong messages without getting seriously checked. Of course, my parents were trying to provide me with the proper upbringing. I remember many times getting into arguments with my mother about my behavioral pattern. But, I was twelve and at twelve who was listening? Certainly not me!

I wanted Nike. I wanted to be cool. I wanted to be accepted by my peers. Instead I wore beat-up, old, grimy, Wrangler jeans that looked as if they were hand-me-downs from my father. My sneakers had no brand name on them and the t-shirts I wore all came out of a ten pack that I shared with my brother, Jimmy. In retrospect, I really didn't look too bad. It didn't help though, that the guy I looked up to, my mentor on the streets, was the local drug dealer. His name was Gilbert.

From the very first day I wanted to be like him. At the age of twenty-one, Gilbert was the type of guy that had it going on: money, power, and respect! All the girls wanted to be with him. To me, he was doing it right. I'd see my father get home from a long day's work too tired for anything. Barely making ends meet. He'd always try to tell me to stay in school and study hard to be able to succeed farther in this life. On the other hand, I listened to everything that Gilbert had to say. He schooled me in the way of the streets and he fed my ego. I respected Gilbert. He talked to me man to man.

My relationship with my mother and father soured rapidly as I became more involved with Gilbert and drifted further away from home and school. For the most part, I hated school.

I actually kind of sucked at it and with that, came frustration followed by boredom. Back then I had no clue as to the importance of an education, so I gave little effort to turn my academic life around. My parents also seemed to give up trying to get me to study and do my homework. I don't know if it was frustration on their part or their lack of knowledge on how to help me overcome what learning disability I had.

Gilbert and his friends became my family—the ones I trusted. They possessed the things I cared about: money, cars, and women. I started leaving school early just to hang out with them and I started to become an integral part of their operation. The first package I delivered for Gilbert was a brown grocery bag held together with packaging tape. It was wrapped as if it was going to be sent by the US Postal Service; each corner meticulously creased and folded. I didn't know the precise contents of the bag, but I figured it was something like money, drugs, or a gun. It didn't matter though. This was a favor for Gilbert.

As I walked to my destination, I found myself thinking about what would happen if I were caught. Amidst my eagerness to help Gilbert I had forgotten that there were cops strewn throughout the Inglewood area. This thought unsettled me, but I would just have to stick to the plan. I would act as if I were innocent and tell them that someone I didn't know gave me five bucks to take the bag to an address. Depending on where I was with my delivery, I would conveniently forget the address and the description of the man who gave me the five bucks. It was simple. *What could they do to a boy?* Just the same, I decided I would deviate from the directions that Gilbert had given me. I knew the area pretty well from riding my bike and hanging out with my younger friends. *Why should I just take the streets?*

Ducking underneath some scaffolding, cutting through back alleys and houses, I made it to my destination: a single level apartment complex. The building was pretty beat up. An old ragged couch sat out in front of the place as if someone had thrown it out ages ago. In the courtyard of the complex, a small built-in swimming pool contributed to the grotesqueness of the building. I walked to the back end of the complex.

Reaching apartment 6-F, I knocked on the door and waited for a reply.

"What's up?" a voice yelled through a small crack in the door.

"I got a package from Gilbert," I replied with confidence, as I tried to sound older than I really was.

The door was pulled inward. I could hear the click of the deadbolt. I could also hear a small safety chain being unlatched. Whoever this was, they were into security. Slowly the door opened. A hand reached out around the door and plucked the package from my hands. I really could not see whom the arm belonged to. Obscured by the angle of the door and the pitch blackness of the room, all I could make out was that the arm of the man was tattooed from the wrist to the elbow. The door closed quickly. For a moment I stood there, confused as if there should have been more. Perhaps recognition of my accomplishment, perhaps a "thank you". I was tripping.

All and all, round-trip, I probably walked a mile to make the delivery. It was no big deal. It had only taken about twenty minutes and I had returned safely. Upon my return, Gilbert gave me a crisp, clean, fifty-dollar bill. Shit, that was love. I hardly did anything and I was paid handsomely in cash.

Later that evening it was like a celebration. My younger friends and I got together and I treated them to everything: ice cream, Bazooka Joe's bubble gum, and video games. Not only did I have the respect from Gilbert and his homies, I also had a lot of respect from my younger friends. Life was great; I had money in my pocket and it was all mine. I had earned it.

The next day, I delivered another package. This time it was a little different. The destination that I traveled to was a lot further than a couple of blocks and the package was a lot heavier. Actually, it was a black duffel bag. It didn't smell like medicine, as the first package I delivered, so I assumed that it was something else other than drugs. *Perhaps it was guns?* I didn't ask and I dared not open the bag to look. It was cool though. It was my job. It was the same as before: a hidden face in the shadows, an arm stretched out to receive the duffel. Once again it went off without a hitch. *This was sweet.* When I returned back to Gilbert, he paid me more than ever before—a couple hundred dollars. He told me that I was turning out to be the best runner to date and that I deserved to share in the wealth. Man, life couldn't get any better than that. Gilbert had baited the line and I took it hook, line, and sinker.

The Rolling Stones' "Gimme Shelter" blared in the background as Gilbert filled his lungs with marijuana. Finishing up his joint, he put a solid mass of cocaine on the table, and broke off pieces in twenty or fifty-dollar amounts. I watched everything that Gilbert did with great intensity. It wasn't before long that I could have easily prepared any concoction that Gilbert made. I could break it up, distribute it, and deliver it. Not only did I watch the mechanics of preparing dope, I was also watching the way Gilbert talked to people. He was always smooth in his dealings with others, and when people tried crossing him, they would be dealt with quickly.

It was a hot, balmy, summer night when I thought all of my good fortune was about to come to a screeching halt. Red flashing lights busted into my bedroom as I heard a siren go off only for a second, followed by a voice transmitted through a loud speaker. "Put your hands on top of your head and turn around," a cop's voice emitted through the bullhorn. With sleep-blurred eyes I stumbled to look at the clock. It was 3:30 a.m.

"What's going on?" my little brother Jimmy whispered.

He too had been awakened by the siren and had climbed up in bed next to me.

"Shhh, I don't know. Just keep it down," I replied.

I tried to remain calm, but I knew that the shit was hitting the fan. Through the blinds I could see Gilbert, kneeling in the street with a couple of his homeboys. *Damn, he was busted.* This was great cause for an alarm to start ringing inside of me. I had seen many times in the movies or on the news where everyone got arrested in the drug bust—everyone from the ringleaders to the henchmen. I figured it was only a matter of minutes before they came knocking on my door. *Isn't that how it worked?* I was picturing myself on tomorrow's five o-clock news. "Get back in your bed and cover up," I whispered to Jimmy. "And close your eyes." I too jumped back into bed and did the same. It never happened. The knock never came. They never broached my door. Within five minutes the patrol car's lights dimmed and slowly drove off—business complete as usual. After they left, I looked out the window for awhile. I didn't have anything else to do and I couldn't fall back asleep. I couldn't believe it. In one fell swoop they had handcuffed Gilbert and hauled my thriving career away.

Next day, I met up with one of Gilbert's girlfriends and got the news. Gilbert had got arrested for 187 on an undercover cop. My jaw dropped and I was speechless. I made my way back home and I began to wonder what I was going to do now. Being introduced to making money in this dope game had me hooked. As I crossed the street to my corner, I was approached by a slow driving car.

"What's up little homie?" said a voice from a '62 Impala that just pulled up.

"Not much," I replied.

Did they know that Gilbert had been busted?

I continued to walk with my head down. The Impala kept an even pace with my stride. I looked up for a second and recognized the passenger who was speaking to me. It was Carlos, one of Gilbert's regular clients, an addict from the word go.

"What's up Carlos?"

"Not much little homie. Hey, you got something for me?"

It was as if a light bulb had gone off in my head. He didn't care if a kid was selling him the drugs. He just needed them, and wanted them bad.

"Come back in an hour," I said. "I'll take care of you."

With that, the Impala drove off.

CHAPTER 2

The first thing I did when the Impala drove out of sight was run like a motherfucker. I was on a mission—a mission that I wasn't sure how I would accomplish. When I finally got to where I was going I was winded. I walked up to four guys who were standing on the street corner.

"Joe, what's up?" I said, as I got about three feet away.

"What's going on youngster? Someone chasing you?" he replied with a slight snicker.

"Can I score some dope?" I asked.

"What happened, Gilbert run out?" he questioned.

Just as I thought: he assumed that Gilbert was low on supply. This had happened before. In the past however, it was Joe who needed some drugs to hold him over until his supply came in and it was Gilbert who obligingly helped him out. I didn't think it would be a problem to reciprocate the favor. "Yeah, that's it," I said, in a scratchy voice. They probably did not know of Gilbert's arrest as of yet. In our neighborhood, Gilbert stayed on his side of town and sold his drugs to his clients. Joe stayed where he was and supplied his people. It was only twelve blocks away, but it might as well have been another country. Neither one treaded on each other's ground. It was a mutual respect that worked well in the view of the bigger picture: to sell drugs and make money.

"How much you need?" Joe asked.

"Let me get a half ounce."

He hesitated for a second. My spider senses started tingling. Yes, even I had an intuition about what was about to happen. For what seemed like a minute, I thought that he wasn't going to give me anything and he would follow it up with a thousand questions about Gilbert. He looked in both directions as if he were about to cross the street. He was looking for cops. "Come with me," he hissed. We moved a few feet away from the group to a neatly trimmed hedge formed of tree shrubs. With his eyes scanning the street, he pulled out a small Tupperware bowl and opened it. Swiftly, he pulled out a small plastic bag that was cinched at the top. "Here, lil' homie, one fifty," he said. I was a little hesitant to verbalize my next request. I really didn't want to handle business this way. I never saw Gilbert do it in this manner and I felt reluctant to deviate from a routine. In lieu of my financial situation however, I had no other choice. Basically my pockets were becoming empty.

"Hey Joe, can I pay you in about an hour?"

"What do I look like, Bank of America?" he asked rather rudely. I froze. I hesitated. I didn't know what to say.

"No problem lil' homie," he said, as he smirked. "I know you're good for it, and besides, I know where you live."

"Thanks Joe," I said, as the tension in my whole body and face began to relax.

Once again I turned on my heels and I was off. I reached my corner within ten minutes. I ran inside my house to the restroom. I began to cut a nice twenty dollar rock. I put it in my pocket and hid the rest in my room. It didn't take but fifteen minutes and Carlos was back, desperate, and needing a fix. The transaction went off without a hitch. I ran back to my room, gathered one hundred and fifty dollars from underneath my mattress, and was off. After paying Joe his money, he smiled. I knew I just sealed his trust for me.

I also maintained one of Gilbert's best clients. Later that weekend while playing basketball at the local park, I met Sal.

Sal was a short guy and he couldn't play basketball worth a lick. He was cool though. For the most part I liked that he was cordial to me and very respectful. Upon first meeting him, I found his demeanor to be rather humble and timid, but as I looked closer I started to learn that this cat had a lot of courage.

"What's your hustle?" he asked me.

"No hustle," I replied nonchalantly.

"C'mon, everybody's got a hustle around here."

I wanted to fuck with him.

"You a cop?" I asked, half goofing around.

"What, are you kidding? I'm fucking 17 years old," he replied. "Of course I'm not a cop!"

I had to laugh. Sal was all right.

"I do some curb selling," I said.

Sal laughed.

"What's so damn funny?" I stammered.

"That's figures," he said. "You hang out on a corner all day just waiting to get busted. You can't be making that much money."

"I do all right," I replied.

"Well listen, I'm doing this thing where your time on the street is minimal and you make a hell of a lot more money."

"Is that right?" I said in a calm, matter of fact tone.

"We're doing carjackings," Sal said.

"Really?"

"It pays a lot more than hustling drugs."

"How much?" I asked.

"Sometimes three grand a night for everybody involved."

"Wow!" I said.

It was a stupid reply. The kid in me was jumping out of my

body. I had trained myself to be cool, but one mention of three thousand dollars and I practically jumped up.

"How can I get in?" I asked.

"Meet me in Culver City at seven and I'll take you with me," Sal replied.

For the rest of the day I couldn't concentrate on anything. My basketball game fell apart and when I returned home, I didn't sell anything. Basically, I just locked myself in my room and waited for night to fall.

Bumming a ride from an older friend, I arrived two blocks away from the park where I was supposed to meet Sal. Walking the rest of the way, I approached the car Sal was sitting in.

"I thought you weren't going to show up," Sal said.

The friendly manner in which we spoke earlier that afternoon had gone directly out the window.

"Well I'm here, ain't I? Let's handle this," I replied.

"Alright then, let's go."

I hopped into the back seat of the 4-door Skylark, directly behind the driver. As the car started to move forward, Sal was already introducing me to Geraldo who sat next to me and Hugo who was driving. As it turns out, Hugo was the oldest out of all of us and had the most experience with this carjacking thing.

"You know how to use a 12 gauge shotgun?" Geraldo asked me.

"Yeah, of course I do," I said, basically lying through my teeth.

"Cool," Geraldo said.

"Well okay, this is the way it's going to go down," Hugo started to say as he flashed glances at me through the rear view mirror.

He was speaking to everyone, but basically the instructions were solely for me.

"I'm going to pull up next to the car that we're going to jack," Hugo said. "Sal is going to cover the driver's side, while Geraldo hits the passenger. You on the other hand, are going to walk to the front of the car."

At this point I was wondering how he was driving, as his eyes never left the rear view mirror.

"Where's my gun?" I asked.

Maybe it was my imagination, but I thought they all turned to look at me as if I was asking a stupid question. Then Hugo passed me a key.

"This will open up the trunk. If something should go wrong, get rid of it. The shotgun stays in the trunk 'till we're ready to go," Hugo said.

"Okay cool," I replied.

We rode the rest of the way in silence. James Brown's "Payback" bumped from the speakers. I had no idea where we were going, but I knew we were not in our neck of the woods. After about fifteen minutes we arrived at the huge parking lot at P.C.H. and Santa Monica Beach.

"Why the beach?" I asked.

There I was again. Asking stupid questions.

They all smirked.

"Think about it man. After a movie or dinner, you want to go hang out at the beach, chill in your car trying to get lucky," Geraldo said.

"And they don't realize that they are slipping," Sal chimed in.

Together they were tag-teaming me with information.

"Before they can bust a nut, we'll have a shotgun pointed at their ass," Hugo said, as he jumped into the conversation.

The Skylark crept around the parking lot like a snail. As if that wasn't suspicious enough, we were doing it with our headlights off.

"Keep your eyes open for something nice," Sal said, as we started on our second lap.

He spoke as if he was addressing everyone, but once again I understood that it was directed as a learning process for me.

"Bingo," Hugo said, in a controlled manner.

All at once we were looking at a silver Isuzu Pup pulling into the parking lot. With low-profile tires and Dayton rims, it was ripe for the picking. Loud music emanated from the windows. Stripping the sound system out of that thing would be very lucrative. Not to mention the money we would get out of his wallet and her purse. *This was it.* Hugo drove and parked about fifteen cars away. Now I was nervous. In the front seat, I could see Sal taking the 9mm out of his belt and placing it between his legs and cocking it.

"You ready?" Hugo said, as he turned around and nudged my knee.

For the first time he gave me a look of confidence, as if to tell me that I could do this.

"Hell yeah, let's do this," I replied.

"Okay, let's do this. C'mon Sal," Geraldo belted out.

Before I knew it, like a well choreographed dance scene, Sal and Geraldo had exited the car while Hugo drove the Skylark directly behind the Pup blocking it in. At first I fumbled with opening my door, but it was only a second before I found my adrenaline pushing me to the back of the car. Sal hit it first. By the time I got the shotgun out of the car I could hear the girl screaming. Racing to the front of the car, I cocked the gun putting the shell in the chamber. The rush of adrenaline made me dizzy and I swayed drunkenly from side to side. It passed quickly, but I actually had to concentrate pointing the shotgun at the right person.

The guy whose car we were stealing was one of those guys we called a *Disco Duck.* He was a Hispanic that wore tapered jeans, a colorful shirt, and long flowing hair that was offset by a crew cut above the ears. He was a softy—a lover not a fighter. Yet, the asshole decided he was going to give Sal a hard time. I guess he was just trying to show off for the girl he was with. *Not very good. Not very intelligent.*

It didn't last long though. As soon as I put the barrel of the shotgun to his nose, he started to cooperate. Like his girlfriend, Sal got him to kneel down facing the ocean. Everything was going according to plan. "C'mon let's go," yelled Geraldo, as he grabbed my arm. That was the queue for Hugo to back up the Skylark. Geraldo and I jumped into the Isuzu Pup. As Geraldo struggled and panicked to get it into reverse, Sal remained outside cool as a cucumber. "Keep facing the ocean," Sal yelled. "And when I tell you, get up and run as fast as you can to the water." Out of the corner of his eye, Sal must have seen the Pup lurch backwards. "Run," Sal yelled.

POP! POP!

Sal had discharged two rounds into the air and we were off. It reminded me of the old gangster movies. I have to say that if there were running boards on the Skylark, Sal would have jumped on them and the whole scene would have been played out in black and white; the Gatling gun smoking from my window, Elliot Ness nowhere to be found.

These romps of carjacking lasted a few months with one happening every two weeks. Everything was successful, everything was fine. That is, until our luck ran out. As we were heading out as usual, trunk key in hand, same game plan as before, just a few minutes from home, we are pulled over by L.A.P.D. We were surrounded at gun point. "PUT YOUR FUCKING HANDS IN THE AIR!" a voice yelled out over the cop car siren. I jammed the trunk key between the seat cushions and raised my hands.

We were arrested and charged with possession of deadly weapons. They found guns on both Sal and Geraldo. Hugo and I had the charges dropped, but Hugo was on probation so he got sent to L.A. County. After a few months in juvenile camp corrections, I was released just in time for my senior high school year. The few months in juvenile camp leveled me out a bit. I didn't care to indulge in carjacking or drug sales. I actually had my mind set for the military. My grades improved and I was one class away from graduating. I got a job at the local Army surplus store and life for me seemed to be on the right track.

CHAPTER 3

It was eight o'clock Saturday night and I just got off work. I rushed home to get ready for the night out. It was eighteen and over night at the Red Onion club. My boys had planned all week for this. It was going to be a night worth remembering. EPMD's "Strictly Business" blasted out the boombox that lay in the corner of my room. My head was bobbing like a pigeon rhythmically to the beat as I buttoned my shirt. I definitely was in a zone. I definitely could feel that I was going to have a good time that night.

At precisely 9:15 p.m. Eric rolled up in his 1989 black Bronco. With jacket in hand, just before I could make my way to the door, I kissed my mother's forehead as she watched her favorite show "I Love Lucy". "Don't come home late," she said, as I walked out the door. I jumped in the Bronco, and we rolled into Inglewood. We picked up John and Jerry. They too were ready to party. Jerry had three Heinekens stashed in a brown paper bag that we would share as we drove over to the club. Shit, I felt like drinking tequila that evening and I hated mixing my booze, but the brew was cold and it tasted good going down. I swigged it several times before passing it on.

We arrived at the Red Onion in West Covina about 10:15 p.m. The place was jumping. We walked in acting like we ran the joint. Most of the crowd were squares and college chicks. All my guys were ex-con, drug dealers, and gangsters. As we got past the front door, a girl with the biggest breasts I have ever seen grabbed Jerry and planted one right on the lips. He pushed her drunk-ass off just in time. Jerry's pseudo girlfriend Vina and her girlfriends walked right in behind us. *Damn, it was going to be a hot night.* We met up with Albert and Big Huey from Venice who already had a table with bottles. Eric and I took a walk to the bar. We ordered shots of tequila. I saw some honeys looking at us and I had every intention of seeing if they would hang out later. The atmosphere in the club that night was electric. You know, where you feel like the music is a movie soundtrack just for you and your actions. Cruising the perimeter of the dance floor, Eric and I could tell that there were a lot of single women there. We maneuvered to where those two girls were sitting, staring at us.

"Hello ladies, my friend and I wanted to ask you a questions," Eric said.

The girls both looked at each other puzzled.

"Hmmm, okay, I guess. Ask away," the first girl responded.

"Do you girls make funny faces when you dance?" Eric asked.

The second girl almost spilled her drink on me from laughing so hard.

"HEY FERNANDO!" yelled Jerry from across the bar. Once he got my attention, he raised his glass and yelled, "¡*Tequila para todos*!" I nodded, raised my glass, and smiled in approval. Yet, in that moment I had a fleeting premonition that the night could possibly be slipping into chaos. Jerry was at the bar getting shit wasted and his girl Vina was dancing alone. At first glance it looked like she was dancing with no one, but I quickly realized that she was gyrating her hips and getting all sexual for someone. Not more than ten feet away stood one of those steroid goon bouncers pretending like he was watching the dance floor, keeping the club ultra safe, when in actuality, he was watching Vina.

What happened in the next ten minutes, I'll probably truly never understand. I should have gone for another drink. I should have gone to the restroom. I should have realized that it was partly Vina's fault for what happened. If she didn't want anything to do with that guy, she shouldn't have been teasing him like she was. *But hell, shoulda, coulda, woulda!* The next thing I knew, the music stopped and Vina decided to strut her stuff right past that guy. Of course he was going to approach her in some manner. I mean, the way she was dancing was like handing him an open invitation. *What was she thinking?* Okay, a gentleman probably would have politely asked her, her name. I guess that is probably what she was expecting, but hell, this was the Red Onion and there were no gentlemen here—just us lions and tigers looking for a piece of ass.

So, this bouncer asshole grabbed her arm like he knew her or like she was his piece of property. Vina took offense to this and slapped his arm away. At first, I found it all quite amusing. If I hadn't had that first shot of tequila, I would have probably been able to predict what was about to happen next and stopped it. The steroid goon, in a moment of rage and rejection, pushed Vina to the ground. That's when shit hit the fan. Like a blur, and to be honest I hadn't the slightest clue of where he came from, John swooped down on the bouncer like a hawk. He dropped him with several lightning type punches. The victory was short lived however, as bouncers seemed to have poured out from everywhere. For a moment, I thought I was Bruce Lee in *Enter the Dragon.* Adrenaline coursed through my veins and I immediately jumped into action.

The first bouncer I came into contact with didn't even see me coming. He probably didn't even think I was in the fight, as he tried to blow by me and attack John. I hit him with a clothesline. The poor bastard, his feet flew up in the air and he busted his head on the corner table. From a few feet away I could see that Jerry and Big Huey had jumped into the action. They looked like they were going to be alright. To be honest, I had other concerns—like how many bouncers were coming out of the woodwork. Whether we could fight or not wasn't the question. We were truly outnumbered.

Before I knew it, I had more bouncers on me and my ass was being thrown outside. Of course they threw a few punches in before I was tossed like a rag-doll onto the cement. Needless to say, Jerry and John followed suit, skidding on their asses. So there we were, the three of us laying on the cement wondering what had happened and asking ourselves the same question: *where the hell was Eric?* As it turned out, he was in the restroom and only saw the end of the scuffle, but never jumped in. Up until that point we were still pretty calm. Pissed off, but calm. There was truly no humility in what had happened; we were all outnumbered five to one. Sure we took our licks and bruises, but we also managed to dish them out in healthy portions. Getting to the car we decided to drive off, but not before we passed the front door. A one hundred percent, bonafide mistake—what happened next, lit the fuse that exploded the bomb.

As the Bronco careened around the corner we found ourselves in a gauntlet of bouncers and others who felt comfortable in numbers. As we drove by, the Bronco was hit with beer bottles that burst on impact, shattering the side window.

"Back the car up!" Jerry yelled.

"What?" Eric said, acting as if he didn't hear Jerry's command.

"He said back the car up!" I yelled.

I knew what Jerry had intended to do and I was on the same page.

"Back it up!" I yelled even louder.

Jerry was already reaching for the middle console that housed the 9mm. I was already rolling down my window. Eric had the tires spinning as the truck leapt into reverse. Now, I don't know if it was the force of the car lurching backwards or the tequila shots that Jerry consumed in the club, but he dropped the gun. It just so happened to land in my lap. I picked it up and aimed. "Fuck you, motherfuckers!" I yelled. Consciously, I wanted to kill. Subconsciously, I probably just wanted to scare the shit out of all of them. At the last minute, I ended up spraying the bullets towards their feet. All I saw were bodies flying everywhere. In the car, we laughed at the sight of all those tough guys jumping and flying like the scarecrow in the *Wizard of Oz*. Not everything in those moments was fun and games. There was still some business to attend to. We knew it was important to ditch the gun. We sped away down Slauson and got on the 605 freeway. When we got on the 405 we turned north. I was relieved that our getaway was so smooth. We had come out unscathed and home safely. Most importantly we didn't get caught. My senses told me another story, however.

For the first couple of days after the incident I walked to work tense. The distant sound of a siren would constrict the lower muscles in my back and my palms would start to sweat. I was just a bundle of nerves. After the third and fourth day, I started to relax. I even became complacent and returned to my old self. I stopped looking over my shoulder and I had become more and more confident that the cops had nothing on us. They didn't have a weapon, a shooter, or a license plate. It turns out that someone did have the license plate and could identify the car. This meant that the threat of an arrest became real. So real, that within a couple of hours they arrested Eric, the driver of the vehicle. With Eric in their custody, they leaned on him hard, and I do mean hard. It turns out that they threatened to dump the charges on him unless he told them who the shooter was. Within minutes he was singing my name and the rest is history.

This wasn't the first time I had fired a gun at someone. This was however, my first time arrested as an adult with heavy punishments.

CHAPTER 4

I felt like I just entered into the waiting room of hell. It was a cold, late night in October and I had just stepped off the L.A. County bus. I walked not as a free man in the free world, but as a prisoner in an unforgiving universe. With my hands shackled to my waist and leg irons holding my feet, I shuffled as I kept up with the procession leaving the bus. With a sheriff deputy to my right and another prisoner to my left, I was just one part of the parade of fifteen men—a parade going nowhere, too soon.

The Los Angeles County Jail is scum of the earth. It's a place where there is no dignity among men and no honor among thieves; where any microscopic piece of love that you still hold in your heart is left at the door and evil is replaced in your soul. It is a decompression chamber for the cesspool of Los Angeles County criminals. For those convicted, it was their holding area until they *caught the chain*. A term used when the transportation bus arrived for sentenced inmates.

Transportation officers would drag several leg-irons by chains. "Open up doors A and B!" the deputy sheriff yelled. I don't have to think too hard to remember the smell as the guard tower pushed the button to open the twenty-foot glass doors. They slid open in opposite directions like those found in a supermarket, but that was the only thing of this experience that resembled grocery shopping. The pungent smell of vomit, body odor, and shit hit us all like a cheap shot to the gut.

The air-con blowing full blast made it like a fridge. The combination of my body perspiring and the thirty degree temperature drop, caused me to burn with fever as influenza began to kick my ass. I tried my hardest to stay alert and wide awake as I waited in line. This wasn't juvenile camp anymore and there wasn't anyone here that gave a rat's ass about me, either. The man I pretended to be ordered me to be stronger. I was eighteen years old, no more than one hundred and fifty pounds, waiting to get fingerprinted and processed into the L.A. County Men's Central Jail.

"C'mon, don't tell me you don't know the drill. Put your finger in the ink and roll from right to left," a White deputy shouted, as he grabbed my wrist and shoved my finger into the ink. Looking up, I could see his face was pock marked and his eyes were flooded with anger. As I looked down and rolled my fingers on the paper, I wondered what evil lurked in the heart of this man. Maybe he hated his job. Maybe his wife hated him. Or maybe he just hated the color brown. I knew he hated me, and without fully understanding why, I hated him.

Wiping my hands in a paper towel, I stepped no further than a yard when another deputy began to release the chains that held my hands and feet together. For one crazy whacked out moment, I thought I was being released. My fantasy however, my utopia, only lasted for a second as reality set in. *Who the fuck was I trying to kid?* This was serious shit and I was in the thick of it. I rubbed my wrist where the cuffs dug into my skin. "Get your fuckin' hands apart," bellowed one of the deputies. Quickly and before I knew it, the cuff on my left hand had been replaced by a white wristband. The kind you get when you're a patient at a hospital. Unlike the ones in the hospital however, where your name is written, where you're someone, where you are treated with respect and cared for, this identification held only numbers.

Like cattle the fifteen of us were herded into what looked like
the laundry room. "Alright, pay up, strip down. We will be handing out plastic bags. Put your belongings in there. They will be
returned to you upon your release," a deputy yelled. A flat-out lie
if I ever heard one because I never saw those clothes again. For a
minute, but what seemed like eternity, I stood there butt-ass naked.
"Turn around," snapped the deputy. Turning on my bare heels, I did
as he said. We all did. "Now bend over and spread your cheeks,"
he bellowed. "I want to see nothing but back doors, wide open!"
To strip me of my clothes was one thing, but this type of inspection
was the worst part.

One by one, a deputy inspected each and every one of us don-
ning plastic gloves and a police flashlight. At the time my naiveté
assumed that he was looking for some type of disease. Later, I
would come to understand that he was simply looking for weapons
or drugs. I discovered where all the shit smell came from: fifteen
motherfuckers bending over every hour on the hour. The guards
threw bars of soap at us. It was this brownish, industrial type of
product that felt like sandpaper. I don't really know what was in
that stuff, but my skin had a direct reaction. Several of the other
guys complained about irritations also. We all wished we hadn't
used it. Upon completion of the shower, I received my bed-roll.
It consisted of: underwear, socks, and uniform, better known as my
county blues.

To process me into the system took most of the night. By 8
a.m. I was booked, but also dead on my feet. This flu was getting
the best of me. The fifteen of us were being escorted down to the
mess hall. Standing in a cafeteria line, I picked up a tray, as I read-
ied myself for some type of meal. To my disgust, what was piled
up on my plate could only be described as what looked like throw
up. Later on, I was told that it was a type of biscuits and gravy

combination. The other inmates called it *S.O.S.,* an acronym for shit on a shingle—an appropriate name.

As far as liquids were concerned they served up this type of punch. I had to admit that it was pretty good. For the first three days, I drank this stuff in order to quench my thirst. That is, until I was told the ingredients. I found out that in order to keep the inmates flaccid, they mixed in a healthy dosage of saltpeter. That was the last I drank of it. Later, I would come to discover that the inmates had nicknamed the punch *Jim Jones.* After breakfast, the few prisoners that were in the mess hall began to disperse. We didn't eat with the general population on that day. Apparently, it took us so long to get booked we missed the regular breakfast. By law however, they must feed inmates three square meals a day and we had our rights. *I had my rights.* Yeah, right!

From there, we were escorted by the deputies to a large escalator. I looked up and down the length of it to register its height. For a minute, it seemed as though it was an optical illusion, as it appeared to ascend at least three stories. I had been in tall buildings before, but none with an escalator that long. It took me by surprise. Placing my foot on the steel grated stairs, my body began to rise; my heart started to flutter and my instincts told me that I was headed no place good. What started off as a coherent ride, passed as a sleep-fogged blur. I vaguely remember following the blue shirt in front of me and my only clear memory of the escalator ride is remembering a couple of lines from a Led Zeppelin song called "Stairway to Heaven". Now, growing up in the hood I listened to hip-hop music. On that day however, the lyrics that kept ringing in my head were from a hard rock band. Not accustomed to listening to that type of music, I could only remember a few lines. They went: "There are two paths you can go by, and there's still time to change the road you're on." I couldn't really remember much else of the song, so I continued to repeat that bit over and over.

How ironic, for I had taken the wrong path and there was no changing the road I was on. Whatever the courts said, I knew in my heart that my acts on the outside were dishonorable and illegal. I had pulled the trigger. There was no innocent man here. I would pay the price. If I came up with excuses of why I was in the system, they would only be tainted by my foolish pride.

CHAPTER 5

W e were escorted to the 9,000 block of module 9,500. From first glance, I could tell it was a shithole; under cleaned, overcrowded, a shark tank full of chaos. Upon entering, I counted around fifty bunk beds, which in my mind, added up to a hundred places to sleep. From what I could tell there were about two hundred guys in there. *This was fucked.*

As I wandered into the module looking for an empty bed, I was approached by an older homie. For a second I thought that he wore a tight, long-sleeved, black t-shirt, but I was quick to discover that it was his skin that I was looking at. He was tatted from the neck on down. Like a live canvas, the black-green lines turned and twisted formulating a mural that expressed power, sex, identity, and beliefs. Inscribed on the left side of his chest was the Roman numeral thirteen in Old English.

"What's your name homie?" he said, in a reserved whisper.

"Fernando."

"Where you from?"

"West L.A.," I said, the words getting caught in my throat.

"How old are you?"

"I'm eighteen."

He lit and dragged a cigarette before he spoke again. The pauses that he took were deliberate. I didn't know if they were for caution or simply how he spoke, but it allowed me to think and imagine what words were coming next. Quite simply, it scared me; I could feel the short hairs on the back of my neck standing up. *Was he friend or foe?* "I'm Hefty. From San Gabriel area," he said. He did not extend his hand or hint any gesture of friendship or warmth. The tone of his voice remained regulated. He presented a matter-of-fact, business type of attitude. His eyes flicked to the left and to the right to see who was watching—a motion of pure instinct. He slowly stubbed the cigarette out on the wall behind me. Once again pausing before he spoke. "Follow me. I'll introduce you to the homies." I followed him as he walked slowly and deliberately.

We passed the first division of bunk beds which were solely occupied by the Blacks. As I trudged along, I could feel the hard stares that we were receiving. I just kept moving. The second group of bunk beds was inhabited by the Whites of the module. Once again, we received nothing but mad-dog stares. We finally reached our Hispanics brothers. We seemed to double the Blacks and the Whites. It was sad to me that my people outnumbered everybody in here; yet I found it comforting to be with so many of my own kind. Unlike the Whites and the Blacks, most of them seemed not to notice or care that I had arrived. As I scanned the room, I could see some of the guys playing cards or chess. To the left, a group in the corner appeared to be gambling by rolling dice.

We stepped toward two guys who were sitting on their bunks. Their faces were angled to a deck of playing cards placed between them. Hefty spoke up. "Sniper, this is Fernando from West L.A." Sniper stood up slowly. He wore no shirt, only his county blue pants. His build was short and stocky. I was surprised to see no tattoos. Switching his hand of cards from right to left, he extended his right hand out of respect.

"*Quvo* homie," he said.

I extended my arm and we shook hands.

"They call me Sniper from West L.A."

"I'm Fernando from West-Los, too," I replied.

From looking at him, I could tell that he was a lot older than me and knowing he was from my area, the Westside, I was certain we would know the same people. "This is Mondo, also from the area," Sniper said, as he gestured over to the other guy on the bed. Unlike Sniper, Mondo was skinny, and covered in tattoos. Under his hardness we were introduced and he smiled a bit.

"Sup homie?" Mondo said.

"Do you need anything? Cigarettes, coffee, how are you on cosmetics?" chimed Sniper.

"I don't have shit," I humbly replied.

"Okay, I'll be right back. Meanwhile, Mondo will show you where your bed's at," Sniper replied.

Before I could respond, Sniper had turned on his heels and was off. "Follow me, homie," Mondo said. I followed him about fifteen feet until we stood at the foot of a row of clean bunk beds. This area seemed cleaner and was mostly Hispanics. "Check this out," Mondo said, as he reached under the mattress and pulled out some new sheets still in plastic. "Are you okay with this tree house?" Mondo asked, as he placed the sheets on the top bunk several feet above his head.

"It's cool," I said, as I looked up. I hadn't realized until that point, but every bunk bed stood at least seven feet high. To get into it, one would have to place his foot on a welded metal triangle at the foot of the bed.

"Here homie, I'll help you out," Mondo said, as he grabbed a corner of the sheet from me.

Together we started making my bed.

"So, what do they have you in here for?" he asked.

"Some punk-ass shooting."

"So, how much time do you think you're looking at?"

"Well, I'm not too sure yet. I'm waiting till I go to court," I replied.

"Yeah, we're all going through the same shit."

Sniper walked up to us.

"Here you go Fernando. It's not much, but I hope it can hold you till you can go to store," Sniper said, as he handed me a small trash bag.

The store in the county jail was a mobile canteen. A huge metal wagon of sorts; it went to every barrack selling cosmetics, tobacco, junk food, and writing material.

"Store comes every Wednesday from ten till two. The limit you can spend is thirty-five dollars. Get the money from your account. You have money in your account, homie?" Sniper asked.

"Yeah some," I replied.

A few minutes later, Sniper and Mondo had resumed their card game and I rummaged through the plastic sack that Sniper had given me. He had grabbed a Snickers bar and cigarettes.

"Thanks Sniper," I said.

"No problem homie," he replied.

"Sniper, Mondo, you want my cigarettes? I don't smoke."

"Shit homie, that's too bad," Mondo said, as he reached up and grabbed them from me. "Thanks homie."

These guys were all right.

Later on that evening, just as I was getting ready for bed, Sniper approached me.

"Fuckin' *Mayates*," he scowled. A *Mayate* is a large black beetle found in Mexico. In prison, it is the nickname that is given to the Blacks.

"What's going on, Sniper?" I asked.

"Stay on your toes, homie," he said. "There's been some tension in the dorm with these *Mayates* over the TV. Never fails, once

NBA playoffs are on, this shit gets crazy! You see, we have a program, and they always want to bend the rules in their favor. The homies want to watch "CALINETE", a Latin version of the Soul Train TV show that's on around the same time as the game. This shit always happens in every prison I've been in. Never fails. You can't trust these scandalous motherfuckers for shit—"

"That's right," interrupted Mondo, shaking his head. "The officers in the podium office watching everyone's movements closely, they too can sense the tension in the dorm."

"Lights out!" a deputy yelled from the intercom. Within a minute the room went black and security lights came on.

"Homie, you good up there?" asked Mondo.

"I'm good homie. *Gracias*," I replied.

Mondo stood up holding a chess board.

"You want to play a few games? I know you ain't about to sleep with all the bullshit going on," Mondo said.

I jumped off my bunk and we set the chess board on top of our locker. You could still see the groupings of Blacks and Hispanics. There was definitely some tension; all the homies still wearing their shoes ready for anything.

CHAPTER 6

To the right of Mondo's shoulder, directly in my eye line, a white sheet started to go up on the bunk a few feet away. I watched as a Black man tucked the sheet under the top bunk and let it drape to the lower bunk as if creating a type of canopy. At first, I assumed that the lights were bothering him and he just wanted to get some more sleep. Initially, I thought that it was a clever idea and that I would use that technique if need be. Then this two-hundred and fifty pound man started to choke this young Black guy in front of him. I still remember the sharp squeal that came from the young guy's vocal cords as the grip tightened down on his neck. It was like chalk on a blackboard.

As quickly as the noise started, it stopped. The large man's grip became so tight that it was impossible for any words to come out of the young guy. Then with one quick motion, the large man's right hand released the young guy's throat and pulled down his pants.

"WHAT THE FUCK?" I whispered to Mondo.

"Don't even fuckin' look that way," Mondo mumbled underneath his breath. "It's none of our business."

The amazing thing was that Mondo never turned around. He never looked back. As if he had eyes in the back of his head, he just knew that some shit was going down. He continued to concentrate on the chess game as if nothing was happening.

The episode lasted for about ten minutes. No one stopped it. No one interfered. It was as though it wasn't even happening. I did my best to concentrate on the chess game before me, but even if I wasn't looking, everyone could hear the screaming. The only way it would come to a halt is if someone of his own race stood up for him—which no one did. "Checkmate," Mondo said, in a nonchalant manner. "Fool, you ain't even paying attention." All I could do was shake my head in an apologetic motion. He was right. I wasn't paying attention. My head was nowhere near the game and nowhere near being a worthy competitor. Mondo knew that. "We'll play tomorrow," he said, as he started to pick up the game pieces. I climbed up to my bed with my shoes still laced up tight, I lay down, still in shock at what I had witnessed. I couldn't sleep, yet somehow I managed to doze off for a few hours. Then a loud voice on the intercom yelled out, "Morning wake up call, prepared for 0-500 chow!"

Over the past few days things seemed to calm a bit. That is, until there was a second incident over the phones. The way it works in County is there are ten phones situated on a wall when you first enter the module. Each prisoner is allowed fifteen minutes for each phone call. The time is watched by a deputy on the catwalk whereupon completion of your fifteen minutes, he hits a button and disconnects your call. It is a rather rude way of ending any type of phone conversation, but it allows every inmate a fair and reasonable chance to use the phone in a particular day. Even with a fifteen minute time span, the lines waiting for a phone could be in excess of three hours. So, if you have the misfortune of getting cut off in the middle of important phone business, you have to go to the end of the line before you can attend to it. A real pain in the ass.

On that particular evening, it was getting near cutoff time for all the phones to be shutdown for the evening. The lines were rather short on account of a nine-thirty cutoff time. It's like a ride at Disneyland when the park is closing: those previous in line will still get to ride and those who arrive after should just find the shuttle to their cars. The last guy in line was a non-English speaking Mexican. In front of him stood a big, fat, Black guy. By contrast, the Mexican guy probably was five feet two inches tall and one hundred and twenty pounds soaking wet.

The Black guy had been on the phone for his fifteen minutes and had been disconnected. Instead of moving out of line and handing the phone to the Mexican, he just stayed there and waited for the phone to reconnect with a dial tone. Basically, he was ignoring the Mexican as if he wasn't even there and was going to use the last fifteen minutes of phone time to make another call. As far as he was concerned, the Mexican would just have to wait till tomorrow to conduct his phone business.

Politely, the Mexican guy told the Black guy his phone time was up and he was next. Already into the second call, the Black guy would have nothing of it and just turned his back on the Mexican guy. For a moment the air in the room went still and the tension could have been cut with a chain saw. As if the module had fallen into complete silence, all eyes fell on the Mexican as he balled his hand into a fist. Cocking it back, he let it fly striking the Black man in the back of the head. *POW!* It was a right hand lead that must of held some power because it pushed the Black man about three feet and struck his head on the wall in front of him.

Everybody who had been watching was surprised. Catcalls began coming from all around the module. The Black man, more dazed and confused than hurt, tried to turn around. *POW! POW!* He was hit with two quick left hooks. The Mexican practically had to jump into the air in order to connect with the Black man's face. Like the Tasmanian Devil, a right and a left followed, as blood started to trickle from the Black man's cheek. Winded and crazed, the Mexican guy threw another barrage of punches before taking a small step back. A mistake perhaps; it gave the Black guy a chance to turn around.

Towering over the Mexican guy, the Black guy now stood facing him with his feet in a fighting stance. Then, without warning and like lightning, the Black man rushed the Mexican and began pounding him everywhere with powerful unrelenting blows. The punches were like a blur as the Mexican was knocked from side to side. With little or no ability to defend himself, the Mexican guy continued to attack. He was getting hit in the jaw, the nose, and both eyes, but he still kept swinging. The Mexican guy just didn't possess the power to compete with the larger man. Then, from out of nowhere, a punch came out of the crowd. So fast it was hardly seen as it caught the Black man square in the jaw, snapping his head back. His legs buckled and it only took him a few seconds before he hit the cement floor of the module. The riot was on.

This was my first encounter with a jailhouse riot. From the look of things I was going to be in the thick of it. It escalated quickly, like a fast moving brush fire, and before I knew it, The Brothers rushed us like a herd of wild animals. Fists and whatever wasn't nailed down was flying everywhere. Mondo stood up on his bunk and shouted, "WHAT'S UP MOTHERFUCKERS?" Then, like a lion, he rushed the oncoming mob throwing left and right hooks at the first Black guy he encountered. For a second, I just stood there. The brawl was right in front of me and there was nothing to do but jump in. Before I could, Sniper ran past me brushing my shoulder.

"Come on Fernando, the first one we get to, we let him have it," Sniper yelled.

"I got your back!" I snapped, as I followed him into the rumble.

PUNCH, KICK, HEADBUTS

Before I knew it, this Mike Tyson look-alike had dropped Sniper where he stood. With two shots to the head, he put Sniper out cold. "Fuck you wet-backs!" he growled, as he looked for his next victim. As our eyes met, it didn't take me long to figure out that he had found one—me. I must have gone into shock; all of a sudden I couldn't move. It felt like I was wearing cement blocks for sneakers and my hands once again felt shackled to my waist. Scenes from my life started to flash before my eyes and I thought to myself that I'm about to get a beating. Deep down in my heart, I knew that all the street fighting I had learned wasn't going to live up to what this guy was going to throw at me. Out of nowhere, Mondo fell from the sky, tackling the Mike Tyson wannabe. With lightning speed, Mondo unleashed a barrage of punches and before I knew it, the Black guy was wedged between the bunk beds. Unable to defend himself, Mondo and I let him have it.

"Okay! Okay!" Hefty yelled from a distance. "That's it, *ya estuvo!*" A term that means "that's enough". "The deputies are coming!" Hefty continued to yell. Then in a flash, canisters of gas came rolling into our area. Instantly, my nose started to run and my eyes began to burn. I took a short breath and my lungs burned as if the air in the module was on fire. A haze of smoke formed in front of my eyes and before I knew it, I started to gag. I looked around aimlessly, but the air was so thick I couldn't even see my hand in front of my face.

"Mondo!" I yelled.

"Right here, little homie," Mondo said, as his groping hand found my arm. "Get low to the ground. The smoke will clear in a few minutes."

Amidst the blackness he pulled me to the floor.

"These fucking pigs are about to raise some hell," he shouted.

He was right. One second later, more than twenty deputies stormed in with riot gear. They were mask protected and ready to whoop some ass.

"What's going to happen?" I hissed at Mondo.

"Just stay alert, these fools can still attack us," he yelled.

In this short period of time we were able to find Sniper and get him close to our bunks. He was confused and disoriented from the blows to his head. The smoke was clearing as we lay him on the lower bunk. The Blacks were the first to get it. One by one they were handcuffed and beaten. Later, I would find out that this was the usual routine after an altercation like this. All in all, it must have taken an hour for them to move us one by one to another dorm. As I surveyed the crowd, I saw Hispanics that were badly injured and being moved to the hospital. One of the guys looked like he was stabbed. Another Hispanic inmate was bleeding profusely from his nostrils. I had to admit that even though they were outnumbered, these Black guys sure held their ground. I sat in the module, hand-cuffed, and wondered where I was going next. For the most part, it was understood that we were also being separated into other dorms. We sat there till two or three in the morning. I was exhausted.

Finally, they got to our group and counted out about twenty men. I was not included with Sniper and Mondo. "Alright then homie, I'll catch you on the rebound," Mondo turned and said to me, as he was escorted from the module. He turned his back and I didn't reply. I never saw him again.

A few other homies and I were led down a long hallway and each put into a one man cell. It was filthy, cold, and it stunk like urine. I was all alone and it was quiet, however. There would be no riot jumping off in here. I paced back and forth, at times standing at the foot of the cell door listening to all the madness on the tier—guys yelling to their homies on the bottom floor and other muffled rubbish.

"COUNT TIME, COUNT TIME," a voice announced from the intercom. Within a few minutes, two deputies walked on the tier to count us by reading our wrist bands. As they got to my cell I stuck my wrist out, as one deputy read it, the other marked a clip board. Once count was over the light are shut off. I sat in my dark cell, just staring at a barely lit, flickering, nightlight. I was exhausted, but for some reason couldn't sleep. So many thoughts crossed my mind. One in particular: I was going to be here for a while. In the distant background, the voice of an older Black man could be heard singing "Tell Me If You Still Care" by the S.O.S Band. I lay there, listening, and fell asleep.

**

CHAPTER 7

It was 4:30 a.m. and I was awoken by a loud voice coming from the intercom. "Chow call!" Then with a click, the cell bars started to open. "Exit your cells in a straight line with your hands behind your back. There is to be no talking or congregating with other inmates or staff," the voice continued to yell. *Damn, I must have fallen asleep. Was it ten minutes? Fifteen minutes? An hour?* I was sleeping so good. Jumping out of bed, I realized I didn't have much time to get ready. So, I got myself together fireman style: rinsed my mouth, wet my face, and dressed in sixty seconds. I didn't fall into line as I should have, but I made it. For a second, I thought to myself that maybe it was going to be a good day.

As I entered the chow hall, I couldn't help but notice everyone sitting in formation as we walked in. The second your group sat to eat, no more than five minutes later, you're asked by the deputies to get up. I got a couple of spoonfuls down my throat then the yelling started again. "Get up. Pick up your trays. Get into single file and exit the chow hall dumping your trays into the dispenser." I unintentionally rubbed my eyes a few feet from the entrance to my cell block.

When exiting your cell, you must be in single file, your shoulder must be up against the wall, and your hands must be behind your back. So, by me lifting my hand to my face, I had committed an infraction of the L.A. County Rule Code. I had made a mistake, but the way they acted you'd think that I had blasphemed every judge, jury, and law enforcement officer in the world. To me, I was just getting something out of my eye. To them, it was breaking the law.

Before I knew it, an officer quickly snatched my hand and my whole body was being slammed up against the wall. With my left hand twisted behind my back, I could feel his left forearm on the back of my neck.

"Oh shit, you're breaking my arm!" I yelled, as excruciating pain ran through the joints that held my arm to its body.

"Shut the fuck up! Who you making signals to, your buddies?" shouted the officer that nabbed me.

My face was pressed up against the cement wall.

"I was just rubbing my eyes!" I yelled.

In that instance, I could see two other deputies approaching the scene. As best as I could tell they were "Jug-heads"; rookie officers straight out of boot camp full of piss and vinegar, ready to do battle. With my face smashed up against the wall and my vision distorted, I could tell that one of the rookies was chewing tobacco. His face was freckled and red. He wore black leather gloves—your typical tough guy redneck. My instincts told me that he was trouble. The other rookie was much heavier, but shorter. The expression that he held on his face was that of great anger.

"What's up with this one, Officer Ted?" the redneck asked, as he snickered. "What the hell did this spic do?"

"We are going to teach this little prick how the rules are taught around here," said Officer Ted.

"Let's show him what we mean, boss," hissed the officer holding me against the wall.

Before I knew it, the two rookie cops were dragging me down this long hall with Officer Ted in tow. The only thing that I could be sure of was that I was in some deep shit. "Where the fuck are you taking me?" I yelled. In the next moment, I was pushed through a laundry elevator door and forced to the ground. The metal edges of the handcuffs dug into my wrists. "You fuckin' cowards," I said angrily. The redneck deputy then kicked me in the back. "Oh shit," I gasped, as pain shot through my shoulder blade. I tried to roll over, but as I did so I caught a boot in my midsection. All of a sudden I couldn't breathe, as the wind was knocked out of me. With my eyes closed, I winced in pain and wondered where the next blow would strike.

For a moment there was complete silence. Then the two rookie cops picked me up to face Officer Ted. "Who the fuck are you to come in here to my house and disobey our rules?" Officer Ted yelled, as a right cross landed on my jaw and knocked me out. A few minutes later I woke up. Being dragged back to my cell. I could hear the homies yelling out from their cells. "Fuck you punk-ass cops! That's some bitch-shit right there! FUCK THE POLICE, FUCK THE POLICE, FUCK THE POLICE!"

CHAPTER 8

The next day was my arraignment. I was awakened at 4:30 a.m. and I was rushed through breakfast along with twenty other guys that also had court. My face and body ached from the beating. By five o'clock we were loaded onto a bus. I sat there, hand cuffed, staring out the window. This sense of joy came upon me knowing we'd be driving through the city. As we exited the jail facility, my mind drifted out the window. How I would give anything to trade places with *that* guy walking his dog or *that* man holding on to his woman at the bus stop enjoying a nice cup of coffee and a donut. It's funny when you realize how much your freedom means to you; when you crave something and simply can't have it.

The bus finally arrived at Pomona Superior Court. Two huge sheriffs armed with shotguns stood by the bus parking entrance. We were escorted out and put into a huge cell. One of the bailiffs approached the cell. "Okay ladies, I'm in charge now," he yelled. "You will do the following, when your cuffs are removed you will walk single file to the elevator where you will wait for further instructions." Our cuffs were removed and we did as he said. Escorted by several deputies, we took the elevator to the third floor. I found out it was the superior court room for high-risk cases. "Exit the elevator and march straight into the bull tank until your name is called," the bailiff yelped.

The bull tank was a holding area for us prisoners as we waited for court. As I entered, I noticed the Blacks outnumbered the

Hispanics. I found a seat on the opposite side of the tank. No one
was talking or saying anything. We were all concerned about our
cases. I knew that most of the guys in here were facing a lot of time.
Court was a tipping point that usually teetered to the undesirable
side for each and every one of us. Then this homie approached me.
Wouldn't you know it? I got stuck with the guy who wanted to talk.
His name was Lil' Boy. I knew that because as soon as my butt
touched the seat, he was introducing himself.

"They call me Lil' Boy from Pomona. What's your name?
Where you from?"

I paused for a moment. The last thing I wanted to do was get
into a lengthy conversation with someone that I would never see
after today.

"I'm Fernando."

"Where you from man, where you from?"

"I'm from the Westside of L.A.," I replied. I didn't even look
at him as I said it.

"Damn, you a long way from home."

I nodded, although I was actually only half listening. Either
he was really anxious about his case, or he was just plain nervous.
I couldn't tell from just looking at him. I thought that we all have a
lot of pent up anxiety however, so I thought I'd cut him some slack
and at least answer him.

"You got that right." I replied.

"Why the hell are you way out here?" he asked.

"An incident I'm accused for happened over on this side of town."

Those were the last words I got in. I guess no one talked to Lil'
Boy no matter where he was—in jail or at home. For the next hour,
he would just spill his guts: I knew what he was in for, how old he
was, when he lost his virginity, what his girlfriend's name was, and
what color his mom's hair was. You name it, he told me. For the

most part, I just sat there and nodded. Lil' Boy was so thirsty to talk that he didn't know I wasn't even in the conversation. Perhaps he didn't care. Finally, Lil' Boy was called for court. "See you 'round," he said, as he got off the bench. Then the strangest thing happened: as soon as Lil' Boy took one step out of the bull tank, he was being shoved back in by the same deputies who had escorted him out. "Hey, what the fuck?" he yelled, as he was tossed back in.

My blood pressure started to rise. Something was wrong. There was a lot of panic happening on the outside. I could see from the mesh steel doors deputies running everywhere. At the time, I had no clue what the hell was going on. Later, I would learn that a riot had occurred in the courtroom downstairs. Some homies and Black guys got into it and apparently it needed the attention of every bailiff, deputy, and attendant to break it up. Realizing what was happening, I started to count. *One, two, three-fifteen-shit, there was twenty of them. One, two, three, four, five*, great, *there was five of us. Fucking great.* We were outnumbered and anyone who could have helped us was downstairs.

"What the fuck is going on?" Lil' Boy yelled.

"Shhh, keep calm," I whispered. "Get ready to move."

"Why?"

At the same time, a voice came across the intercom. "All the Blacks, put your faces up against the wall, hands over your heads." Now, it really doesn't take a mathematician to figure out what was happening. The voice on the intercom meant, one bailiff on the intercom, all deputies downstairs, zero deputies on our floor, twenty Blacks against five Hispanics. A fight. *Yeah right*, more like a massacre.

"Fuck the Mexicans!" a Black Crip yelled out. I could tell that he was a Crip because he had blue rubber bands that braided his hair. He turned his body around and the rest followed suit. They rushed us; nowhere to go but cover up. "Stand down! Stand down!" a voice yelled from the intercom. Seconds later pepper spray canisters and masked deputies charged in take control. Quickly, we were moved to an empty bull tank downstairs. We all needed medical attention, but not given any. I was bleeding from my nose. The shiner on my left eye was completely shut. I walked to the sink to clean my face. A few minutes later a deputy returned to our cell tank. "Rocha! Exit the cell, you have court." I sighed. My head was still throbbing and I knew there was no getting out of this. *How would I tell my family that I was okay? How could I tell them not to worry?*

As I entered the courtroom my sisters started screaming and crying all at once. I got a glance at my mother as the deputies were guiding me to my chair and she was sobbing hysterically.

"Oh shit. What happened to you?" my court appointed lawyer asked. I didn't even turn to look at him.

"Son, what happened to you?" the judge asked, towering over the courtroom, wrapped by a ton of finely varnished oak. "Are you okay?"

"Yes, sir. I'm fine," I replied. "I slipped and fell."

"I've heard that one before. Let's proceed with the case."

With much prestige and dignity, he lifted his glasses onto his face and started reading the charges set against me. Finishing, he finally asked me how I would like to plead. At that moment I got such a lump in my throat as I looked up with a blank expression. "Not guilty," I replied. Some back and forth legal gibberish between my lawyer and the prosecutor went on. I couldn't help but look back to see my family, eye's watery and forcing a smile for me. I too forced one back.

CHAPTER 9

M y first day in court and ironically enough, all I could think of was returning to County and laying my head on my bunk. On the bus ride back, reality started to set in. It didn't matter that less than an hour ago, under my lawyer's advice, I pleaded not guilty. That would provide the smoke screen for the courtroom antics that were to follow; with the judge as king of his court and with my lawyer as the court jester. For the D.A., there was just a small puzzle to figure out and prove that I was guilty. For my lawyer, it was up to him to fight for the best deal possible.

My life became a repetition of the day before. I would wake up at 4:00 a.m. and I would be rushed to the mess hall to scoop down some breakfast. By 5:00 a.m. I would be loaded onto the bus where I would take the long, but always the most enjoyable part of my day, bus ride. By 7:30 a.m. the bus would roll up to the Pomona courtroom where I would be escorted to the bull tank to wait—and waiting is what I would do. Sometimes, I didn't get called into court at all. Those were the dry runs—when someone was missing. Some of the days the D.A. wouldn't show and on other days the judge would take off. I was the only one that had to be there. After court, I would be returned to the bull tank to wait until every case was heard. That usually was about 8:00 p.m. After spending the whole day in the bull tank, just bored out of my mind, I would board the bus for the long trek home. It would be about 11:00 p.m. before I got back to L.A. County and back in my cell.

Too often though, I would have to endure sleepless nights. The racial wars between Mexican and Blacks were no joke. If I did sleep, I was averaging about four hours a night. Near the end of my court case, I was starting to look like a raccoon on crack. Even the bags under my eyes had bags. My body was filled with exhaustion and my heart was filled with despair. So, for months this was my life: up at dawn, court all day, bull tank till night-time. The excitement and the anticipation of it all was almost too much. Then one day it all came to a screeching halt—the day of my sentencing.

I was escorted to the courtroom for the last time, in the same suit that I had worn throughout my whole trial. I thought that every-body would notice my heart beating through my chest. As I entered the courtroom, the jury was leaving. They were being escorted by a bailiff to a separate door opposing my end of the room. I knew from my newly gained knowledge of courtroom procedure that they had already read their verdict to the judge and the D.A. They had al-ready written my destiny and there was nothing I could do about it. The courtroom was full of cops, lawyers, and all my immediate family members: my mom, my dad, Jenny, Cheryl, and my little brother Jimmy. I smiled towards them as if to let them know I was okay. My mom and my sisters were all crying. I did my best to choke my tears back. I wanted to be strong for all of them.

"All rise," a bailiff cried out. "The honorable judge Hartman presiding." The whole courtroom stood up for all the formality as this man in a dark robe entered. I stood with everyone. As everyone took their seats my lawyer whispered to me to remain standing. "All courts presented here," the judge said. "In the case of Rocha versus the State." When he said that, he looked up from the docket he was reading and stared me straight in the eyes. "I'm now going to read the verdict to you Mr. Fernando Rocha. Then I will read you your sentence. You have the right to speak after the sentence has been given to you. Do you understand?"

"Yes," I replied.

"Well sir, from the charges of attempted murder and the assault with a firearm, this court finds you guilty on all charges. I sentence you to no more or less than ten years in the California Correctional Facility," the judge announced.

Fancy jargon for the state prison.

As he read my sentence, I could hear my sisters and my mother crying. I myself was using all the energy in my body to hold it in. I did not want to break down. *Not here, not like this.*

"Do you understand, sir?" the judge asked.

"Yes, I do," I replied.

"Do you wish to say anything before I dismiss the case?"

"Yes, sir."

As I stood, I turned away from the judge who was speaking to me, away from the court that had just sentenced me. I turned and faced the ones who loved me the most, the one who loved me through my childhood and put up with me through my wild teenage years; even in that moment, as I stood as a criminal, I could still see the love they held for me in her eyes. I faced the people I had hurt the most—my parents. I uttered *perdon,* I'm sorry.

"Turn around and face the judge, son," a bailiff yelled. "You're out of order."

I turned and looked at him as hatred burned in my eyes. I could have killed with a mad-dog stare.

"I'm done. I have nothing more to say," I said with more composure.

"Well then, remove this man from my court," the judge said, as he slammed his gavel onto his desk. "Well son, take good care."

I turned to see my lawyer standing there, his hand held out prepared to shake my hand.

"Fuck you. You dump-truck bastard," I hissed under my breath.

"Okay, that's enough, come with me," the bailiff to my left shouted as he grabbed my arm.

At that point, I could still hear the sobs coming from the part of the room where my family sat. I didn't want to upset them anymore than they were, so I wasn't about to make a scene. On the inside I was boiling over with hatred. On the outside I wanted to remain calm, cool, and collected, and give my family the impression that I was going to be just fine. Before I left the courtroom, I glanced back and all I could see was my sisters' face covered by tissue and my mom's head nuzzled in my father's shoulder. I could see that they were taking this real bad and the worst thing was I could do nothing to resolve their pain. Knowing I was the cause of it was the worst.

I was immediately taken to a different holding cell. This room was fully covered wall-to-wall in soft white cushion. Even the floor and ceiling was covered with plastic-type gym mats. Not one piece of hard cement was exposed.

"What the fuck's going on? Why am I being put in here?" I asked.

"This is just procedure. Just relax, it will only be for a couple hours," the bailiff answered me.

"But I'm not crazy. I don't belong in here. Why can't I go back to my tank?" I said. "I'm not crazy."

The ironic thing was I was yelling like I was out of my mind. I thought, that *they* thought I was crazy, otherwise why would they have put me in this rubber room? Later, I would come to learn that this was called the "cool down tank". It was a cell that they would put guys into who were sentenced to heavy time in order to simmer down. I was angry, but I wasn't going to bang my head up against the walls. Realizing that there was really nothing that I could do, I started to look around. Like every other place that they locked me up, this place was filthy. A lot of the cushion had blood stains on it. If not blood stains, it was marked with snot or spit. I found the cleanest spot to sit down. After about ten minutes, I started to realize that this place really wasn't that bad: for one thing, it was quiet and it really didn't smell too bad, and this clean spot that I had found was quite soft. Closing my eyes and laying flat, I fell asleep.

So, for the next month or so, it was business as usual in County—a never ending maze of chaos. After returning from my sentencing, I was placed not in a single man cell, but in module 3400-Baker Roll. Like before, I hooked up with my Hispanic brothers. To pass my time, I played chess with this old timer. His name was Old Man Joe. He was a rather thin, crusty old man that liked to win and usually didn't want to stop playing until he did. Joe was fifty-five years old and had been in and out of prison from the time he was eighteen. He was a heroin drug user.

At lights-out, when it was too dark to see the chess pieces, Old Man Joe would tell me old prison stories, or give me advice on how I should behave once I got transferred to up state prison. As I lay on my bunk, I listened with great intent. Some of the stuff I already knew, but the things I didn't know, and the ground rules that he schooled me on, I would use for the rest of my prison life.

Often, Old Man Joe would make me take out my identification card that we had to carry with us at all times. On the left hand side of the laminated I.D. was my mug shot. Old Man Joe would always ask me whom I saw on that card. My reply would be that it was just me. Then he would ask me if I saw anyone else's picture on my I.D. Of course my reply would be a stern "no". Then just like the night before and the night before that, he would say, "Remember son, just do your time and no one else's."

So, it was Thursday, and Old Man Joe and I were once again involved in a heated match.

"Okay lil' homie, it's your move," he said.

"Okay, okay. Hold your horses, you old battle-cat. I'm trying to think."

I smiled at Old Man Joe as I moved my queen into a check position.

"Oh, hell," he replied as he looked down at his chess pieces to contemplate his next move. He never got to make it.

"Washington 1-8, Reid 4-0, Rocha 1-3" a voice announced.

"Oh shit, that's me," I replied.

I didn't hear the rest of the names being called, but what was said next was clear as a bell.

"Roll your shit up. You're being transferred. Tehachapi," the deputy continued to yell at the doorway.

"Well, what the fuck you waiting for?" Old Man Joe asked. "Go get your shit ready."

"Damn," I said. "It's about time."

I think I was a bit in shock. Finally, I would be leaving this hell-hole. What I didn't know is that my hell was just beginning.

"Hey Joe, it's too bad we didn't get a chance to finish our chess match."

"Don't worry about it youngster, I hope we can one day, but out on them streets," he replied.

He reached out and shook my hand. I said my goodbyes to a few friends that I had just met and some of the guys I had known for awhile. I brushed by Old Man Joe one more time as I gathered my things. "Stay up youngster. Remember, one picture in your I.D. card!" he said, as I walked away from him.

CHAPTER 10

The bus ride up to my next stop was about three and a half hours long. From the best I could tell we were headed north. I was happy to be leaving that shit-hole County. I never wanted to see its ugly face again. The bus ride was pretty relaxing. Like all the other times, I tried to take in as many views as I could from the outside. The sun beat on my face as I stared out the window.

About three hours into the ride, the road narrowed. We drove right through a small town. A few more yards down the road however, I could see what looked to be a trailer park. From a distance they looked old and run-down, but as I got closer they really didn't look too bad. What little landscaping they had seemed well groomed and the trailers themselves seemed to be clean and well taken care of. I would have given anything to be dropped off right there. In the same section, by the side of the road, several male Native Americans were selling their goods. These merchants looked at the bus as it drove by, with blank stares. They knew where we were headed and I knew in their hearts they did not envy us. On the other hand, children ran in the background and I couldn't help but wish to be them; to have my youth and innocence back, to be a child once again without a care in the world. If only I could have comprehended how much freedom I had at age ten, instead of being hit with the reality of how little I had now at the age of eighteen.

I looked up at the two Correctional Officers (C.O.'s) that were in the bus with us. From the look of them, they didn't look much different than the deputy sheriffs I left behind in County. The only difference I could tell was that they seemed to treat us with much more respect. I couldn't figure it out, but something was different.

At about one in the afternoon, we arrived at my new home, the California Correctional Facility at Tehachapi, C.A. I felt like I was in a real movie. As the bus drove up, all I could see for miles around me was desert. In front of me, like a mirage, a huge building made of concrete started to appear. As we got closer I could see that it was surrounded by a large fence topped off with barbed wire. Later, I would come to find out that it was several fences that I was looking at, three deep to be exact. What really blew me away was when I found out that each one of those fences was charged with electricity.

I was in the front of the line of my group to step off the bus. Six of us shackled together like a six pack of beer; the heat and the humidity blasting me in the face. Every single one of us shuffled through the compound. From there we were put into a large cage with some other guys who looked like they had been in there for a long time. At least overnight. This was the holding area where we would wait until we were processed into the system. That is where I met Smiley.

"Hey, what's up man?" I asked, as I introduced myself to him. "I'm Fernando from West L.A."

"*Quvo*, I'm Smiley, from the Eastside. I've never been to this prison before," he said after a short pause.

I guess he was just thinking of something interesting he could tell me.

"It's brand new," he continued.

"I guess you've been around the block once or twice before?" I replied.

"Yeah, I did a short bid in Folsom, back in 89."

He really didn't tell me where he'd been since then and I wasn't asking. Smiley was a lanky dude that stood over six feet tall and he wore a full long mustache like Yosemite Sam.

The unique thing about him though, was that he had a super high pitched voice like Mickey Mouse. At first, I wanted to laugh, but I think it was because of his voice that I took a liking to him. *How could someone with a voice like that be all that bad?* He surely didn't intimidate me with it. "Everybody, as I call your name, get into a single file line and walk with me to your new cell!" a C.O. bellowed.

"That's us homie, let's go see where we are going to live," Smiley said, with a little too much enthusiasm. We walked outside to a fenced-in area. In the center of this area was a huge yard. From my first view of it, it looked to be about two hundred yards spanning in each direction. Looking through the fence and into the yard, all I could see was a gang of men looking at us; staring us down, trying to figure out who we were, seeing if they could recognize a familiar face among us. I walked behind Smiley and tried to not look conspicuous. Looking up and a little bit to my right, I noticed one of the many gun towers there. It had the most noticeable and always present, six foot, three hundred pound guards that chewed tobacco and carried Mini-14 assault rifles. It would be an image that I would see time and time again.

As we walked around the track, inmates were being paired off and sent into different buildings. When we got to building five, the last building, Smiley and I were the last ones left.

"It looks like we're the last two. Maybe we'll get to be *cellies*?" Smiley whispered over his shoulder.

"That'll be cool," I replied.

I was hoping I would get Smiley as my cellmate. He seemed pretty cool. He didn't seem crazy or too intimidating and he seemed like he knew the system. Sure enough, two seconds later, we were walked into building five and put in the same cell. The day was looking good. Immediately, we unpacked our stuff and made our beds.

"Hey homie, I'm going to get into the yard and get some sun, you coming?" Smiley asked, practically jumping out of his skin.

"I'll be there in a minute. I'm going to try and use the phone and let my folks know that I'm okay."

"I understand homie. I just haven't been in the sun since I can remember."

That day I didn't get the chance to take in any sun or talk to my folks. By the time it was my turn to use it, it was chow call. I walked to form a line out of the cell block. Walking out to the yard along the track I met up with Smiley. We continued to walk towards the mess hall. "I met a few guys I was in Folsom with. They said for us to come out to the yard tonight and they would introduce us to the fellows," Smiley said, as we slowly made our way to the mess hall. Getting our food, I was a bit shocked. I could actually tell what the food was. It was meatloaf. I was actually even more shocked when I tasted it. It was actually pretty good, unlike the slop they served in County.

"Damn, I haven't had a decent meal like this in over a year," I said.

"The food in here is fresher. Besides, it is cooked by inmates and not machines," Smiley said.

Finishing lunch, Smiley and I walked back to our cell. He seemed to be settling in comfortably as he hoped up on the top bunk. Lying on his back, he crossed his feet and folded his arms across his chest.

"What you doing homie?" he asked, as he stared at the ceiling.

"I don't know. I really could use a shower."

"Well go homie. What you waiting for? This ain't County. We're allowed to shower more than once a week."

I collected my cosmetics in order to take a shower. As I closed the cell door, I noticed Smiley was snoring and knocked out already. I showered for what seemed like an eternity.

The limit was fifteen minutes and later I was informed that the rule wasn't strictly enforced. No one really cared just as long as no one was waiting for the shower. The water was hot and steamy. I got myself all lathered up and cleaner than I had been in months. The relaxing thing about these showers was that they were one-man showers. They had cell bar doors. Not exactly private, but a hell of a change from the piss-hole that one had to shower in at County. Best of all they were *clean*.

Later that night, Smiley and I went into the yard to meet the fellows. Lock up was at eight o'clock, so the inmates still had time to be in the yard. As I walked outside, I felt a sense of joy. The cool breeze and the night smell was so refreshing. If not for the barbed wire fence, I could probably have imagined that I was camping. As I looked up, I could see a billion stars glowing in the night sky. I couldn't believe how many of them were up there. I couldn't remember when I last saw the moon. The whole experience was satisfying.

"Keep *trucha*," Smiley whispered, as we approached the other homies in the yard. *Trucha* was a prison term, meaning to be aware.

I immediately stopped looking upward, as I forced my attention to the men in front of me. Even though they were Smiley's friends, it didn't necessarily mean that I didn't have to keep my guard up. As we got closer, one of the older inmates from the group split up and approached us. Showing proper prison etiquette, his move towards us was cautious and his voice was calm, but stern.

"Hey, what's up homies," he said, in a rather quiet voice.

"What's going on?" Smiley replied. "Dreamer, this is my cellie, Fernando. He's from the Westside."

"What's up?" I said, as I stuck out my hand for him to shake it.

"These are the fellows," Dreamer said, as he started making his way over to the group.

He rattled off six names, one for every inmate. Unfortunately, my short-term memory didn't remember any of the guy's titles, but I shook their hands with respect and appreciation. I realized that these were Smiley's friends, his immediate homies from East L.A., so I didn't hang out for too long. After about five minutes of small talk and as the conversation started to stall, I politely excused myself.

"It was good meeting you guys. I'm gonna walk. I'll catch you later Smiley," I said.

"Okay Fernando, I'll see you later."

As I walked alone and around the large walkway that surrounded the middle of the prison yard, I was amazed at the complexity of this place. As I checked things out, I noticed how everything seemed like a little town all to itself; a little city surrounded by nothing but sand, totally self-sufficient from the outside world. Pretty amazing. Within the walls, there were Blacks and Whites segregated from each other. Within the large community of Hispanics dwelling here, there were also two groups that were segregated. They were the Northern Mexicans and the Southern Mexicans.

As I kept on walking, I came upon a little fenced-in area. This looked like the weight pile. The equipment looked older than dirt. Bars were bent and some of the benches were rusted. After what seemed like a couple of laps around the yard, I was drawn to a handball game. I never played the game, I didn't know the rules, and I never saw the local guys at home batting a little rubber ball around, but for the most part I thought it to be a game for the old-timers.

At the moment however, two young Hispanic cats were involved in an intense game as they swatted at the ball with lightning speed. It occurred to me that this was not a game for senior citizens, but for someone who had a lot of athletic skills and stamina. The level of competition in this particular game was almost intoxicating. Both guys played with full emotion—not giving up until victory would be theirs. I was immediately intrigued by the sport. I wanted to play.

I wanted to learn. I wanted to be part of the action. For now, I would just watch.

BUZZZZ! BUZZZZ! BUZZZZ!

My first instinct was to cover my ears. A loud buzzing sound resonated throughout the yard. Like a fire engine that had gotten out of control it rang like crazy nonstop. I noticed every inmate in the yard diving to the ground. I was a bit slow in those days because I was the new guy, but it didn't take me long to follow suit. I think it was a half a second later and I was hitting the ground. "DOWN ON THE YARD, GET DOWN!" a voice bellowed from an intercom. The next thing I heard was a gun shot. I had no idea where it came from or where it was going. I had my hands over my head and my face buried deep in the dirt. I found out later that it was a shot aimed at the men to break up a fight on the basketball court. Back in the day, if a fight or a riot broke out they would throw on the annoying intercom. Then they would fire a warning shot into the air.

If you are in a fight now, you must stop as soon as you hear the buzzer because they do not send out a warning shot anymore. In fact, there are painted signs all over the walls with the same verse, "Warning. No warning shots".

On that particular night, the C.O.'s immediately took control of the situation. One man shot in the leg and both men faced new charges. Within seconds the incident was handled. Minutes later, like it never happened, inmates were getting up and it was the normal program as usual: the basketball games started up again, the weight lifters once again started grunting and pumping iron, and the handball game resumed. I slowly picked myself up and dusted off my clothes. This was the first time I had ever encountered a situation where an inmate got shot for fist fighting. I sighed and thought to myself that I had enough of fresh air for the evening and headed back to my cell-block.

In prison, you get fifteen minutes every hour to get in and out of your building or your cell until lock up time, which is at 10 o'clock. After the fifteen minutes, you are stuck where you are. I arrived at the cell, just before they were ready to lock it down again. I was alone. Smiley had not come back yet so I took that time to settle in some more. My precious belongings consisted of my cosmetics, a dozen or so snapshots of friends and family, a few letters from an ex-girlfriend of mine, and a little tiny Bible given to me by the L.A. County chaplain. During the next fifteen minute unlock, Smiley returned.

"What you doing, homie?" he asked.

"Just looking at some photos," I said, as I turned them to show him.

"Damn, she's fine," Smiley remarked with excitement in his voice. He was pointing at a snapshot of Vina wearing a tight tank top and a pair of daisy-dukes. "Who's that?"

"That's my homeboy's lady," I replied.

"Damn, she's fine," he said. "Can I get her address?

"Nah, I don't play that shit, fool!" I said.

"Okay, I understand homie."

Immediately, he started shifting his belongings around.

"But she sure is a beautiful girl," he said.

"Yeah, she is a hot one," I said.

I had to agree.

CHAPTER 11

In the first week, all the new guys had to go through medical checkups. They probed, we coughed, they tapped, we pissed, and then they drew blood. They were checking for T.B., AIDS, and whatever else you could think of. Passing the physical gave you privileges like the other inmates. Once you were cleared you'd be eligible for a job, able to receive mail, care packages, visits, and be eligible to use the phones.

There were four phones in my building: one for the Whites, one for the Blacks, and one for the Mexicans. The last one was communal, meaning any race could use it. On that particular phone, a policy of courtesy had been instated long before I got there. For example, if a Black guy was using that phone, I would politely ask him how much longer he was going to be. He might respond with telling me he would be ten or fifteen minutes longer. I then would say that I would get it after him. Now, even if one of his Black brothers came up to him after me and wanted to use the phone, he would extend the courtesy of giving it to me first. I then in turn, would extend the same courtesy to the Black guy before giving it to one of my homies. It is how that phone worked.

I must have waited at least forty-five minutes to make my first phone call home. My dad answered, he was the only one home at the time.

"Hey *mijo*. How are you doing?"

"I'm okay," I replied.

"We all miss you very much."

I got a little choked up as he said that. My dad was never much for showing me or expressing any emotion. By telling me he missed me, even though he expressed it by saying my whole family missed me, meant a lot. Most of the time, I couldn't read between the lines, but this is one of those memorable moments when I did. It touched my heart that he went at least this far to tell me I was in his thoughts.

"Your mom can't sleep at night. She has nightmares that something bad is happening to you," he said.

"Tell mom not to worry. I'm okay, and I'll call her next time I get a chance."

"*Si Mijo*, I'll tell her. Be careful and take care."

My dad hung up so fast, I didn't even get the chance to tell him goodbye. *Did I think something would change?* That was just him, never the type to be too sentimental. It made me sad as I walked away from the phones. Not because it took me almost an hour to make that fifteen second call, but because I wished we were closer. I wished I could have laid some of my burdens on him and truly talked to him. That never was our relationship however, and it wasn't about to change any time fast. Over the next few months I was getting well adjusted to the program here at Tehachapi State Prison. As a few weeks went by, I would exercise in the mornings when the yard opened up. I was getting cut and ripped. For the first time in my life, I had a six-pack.

I was writing a letter when Smiley walked into the cell from yard. He didn't look good.

"Hey homie, what's up? What's wrong? You look like you've just seen a ghost," I said.

"What? Umm, umm, nothing's wrong," he replied.

I could tell something was up. Smiley was acting skittish. He looked up at me and I saw a frighten man. Hell, if Smiley didn't want to talk, I wasn't going to force it out of him.

"You going out to night-yard?" I asked.

"No, think I'll stay in today. I have some letters to write," he said.

An hour or so later the cell doors opened and a loud voice on the intercom yelled out, The yard is open!" I left without saying anything else.

My concerns over Smiley's attitude grew for the next few days. Nothing that I could do or say would pry Smiley loose from his cell and he would always make up some lame excuse of why he wanted to stay in. One day, he told me he needed to catch up with his legal work for his appeal. The next day he said he needed to write some letters. It didn't matter that it was eighty degrees and sunny, he just wouldn't budge. So, for the third day in a row, I went out to the yard myself.

My lungs ached as I completed three miles along the inner track. The desert sun beat on my back and I could tell that today was going to be a hot one. With my shirt, I wiped my brow and then I bent over to gasp for more air. As I looked up, two huge guys were approaching me. I was hoping that they were going to walk around me because they were the type that you really didn't want to deal with. One of the guys wore a muscle shirt. The skin that was exposed was fully tatted down. The other guy wore a state issued blue button-down shirt. Even though it was hotter than hell in the yard that day, both of his sleeves were buttoned tight around his wrists and to keep up with his gangster image, only his collar button was snapped shut. On his stomach, he had a large tattoo that read "Brown Pride". Both were corn-fed and muscular, much larger, and much more intimidating than my hundred and fifty pound ass.

"Hey youngster, can I talk to you for a second?" the guy in the muscle shirt asked.

Damn, they weren't walking around.

"Yeah, what's up?" I replied.

"Is Smiley your cellie?"

"Yes," I answered.

"All right, thanks," he replied.

Before I knew it they had turned on their heels and started walking the other way. I was quite surprised. I started to wonder if they had anything to do with why Smiley is acting so strange. I walked back to my cell. I wanted to get to the bottom of all of this. As I walked into the cell, Smiley quickly jumped up and greeted me. He also had his boots on as if he had somewhere to go. I found this quite odd because in the past Smiley never got up for no one and the whole time he was in the cell his shoes would be off.

"What's going on, homes?" he asked.

"Not much," I replied. "What's up with you?"

"Not much. Reading."

There was a long pause before anything else was said. I purposely held back from saying anything. It wasn't really my business to pry and I wanted to see if Smiley was going to spill any information. As it turned out however, he *was* waiting for me to say something. So I did.

"Hey, two guys in the yard asked me if you were my cellie."

"Oh yeah, did they say anything else?" he asked.

"No. That's pretty much it and then they walked away."

"Are you sure they didn't say anything else?" he asked, as he eyed me suspiciously.

"Hey, what do you think, I'm lying?"

I was starting to get angry. Everything was very confusing and I was tired of this little cat and mouse game that Smiley was playing with me.

"I'm sorry homes," Smiley said.

There was a short pause.

"Hey, by the way, what did these two guys look like?" he asked.

I described both of them as best as I could. As I did so the look on Smiley's face went from seriously worried to absolutely scared shitless. His shoulders drooped and his face went positively red.

"Hey, well, look Fernando, people are going to say shit about me to you. It doesn't necessarily mean they are telling you the truth. I told you before the whole prison system is full of shit." He paused momentarily; ever cautious of the words he was choosing. "Now, Fernando, these guys are probably going to say stuff about me that is not true. I mean they probably don't know the whole story. They've probably just heard part of it."

I nodded. I kind of understood what he was talking about.

"They're going to say shit to you, but be your own judge. Weigh the facts before you come to your conclusion. Don't let them persuade you in any way."

"Like what kind of stuff?" I asked.

"All kinds of bullshit," he replied.

"Look Smiley, I'm your cellie. Be straight-up!"

He sighed one of those big long sighs before he started speaking.

"Look Fernando, its okay you don't have to worry. I'm not scared of those guys. My past is just catching up with me. It's happened before in other prisons. It's no big deal, I just take a beating then I transfer to another prison and start all over, till someone from the past recognizes me again."

I nodded and waited for him to speak some more.

"Fernando, I'm no rat and if that's what they think, fuck them. They don't know the story," he said.

"Smiley, what the fuck are you talking about? What's this shit about being a rat?" I asked.

"They didn't talk to y—"

I interrupted him. "Like I told you before, they didn't say shit. They just asked me if you were my cellie. Now, tell me, what's the deal with you?"

"Alright Fernando, but only because you're my cellie and you're a good guy."

"I'm listening," I said.

"It was late October of '89 and my cellmate and I were arguing about some crazy bullshit. Then we started to exchange blows. When the C.O.'s broke it up they ram packed our cell and found a *shank*."

A *shank* was a term used to describe a type of knife.

"So, when they asked me whose it was, I told him it wasn't mine," Smiley said, in a desperate voice. "Then they asked me if it was my cellie's and I told them that I didn't know. So, I told them, 'why don't you motherfuckers ask him?' I guess that was enough for them. They said for being a smart ass that they were going to tell him that I said it was his and that they were going to charge him with carrying a concealed weapon. So, that's what they did."

"That's some fucked-up shit, man," I replied. "Why didn't you tell your cellie they set you up?"

"He wouldn't have believed me. It only took a second and the damage was done."

"Well, check it out Smiley, I don't want no problems. Whatever you and those dudes got going on, it's none of my business," I said.

That night I could not sleep one bit. Most of me didn't believe Smiley for shit. The other part of me didn't know what to believe. *Was I anxious about the whole situation? Did those two big motherfuckers scare the shit out of me?* Maybe. All I really knew was that I was tied into this situation simply because I was his cellmate.

The next morning, I went to breakfast alone. I tried to wake Smiley up, but he just rolled over and fell back asleep. Most of the guys in the cellblock already knew what was going on with Smiley. I felt the stares and the tension as I entered the chow hall. It seemed like I was the last one to know and the last one to find out. That morning I sat alone. That is, until the two guys who approached me in the yard came to sit with me.

"So, where is Smiley?" the guy in the muscle shirt asked.

"He's still in his cell asleep," I replied, with a scratchy voice.

"That piece of shit has to roll it up," said the second guy, as he knocked twice on the table.

The guy in the muscle shirt in an attempt to keep the situation calm placed a hand on the arm of his partner. Then he turned to me.

"Listen youngster, you don't know us, we really don't know you, but we and the people we are associated with could really use your help." His voice was calm and very matter of fact. "Check it out, homes," he said. "It's like this, Smiley fucked up back in Folsom. He ratted some guy out from the mob and he needs to be dealt with in the proper manner ASAP."

"So, what do you want with me?" I responded.

I didn't know if my face shared more fear or confusion.

"Well, since he is your cellie, it's only right for you to take care of him. You're the only one who can get close to him and since he has already seen us, he's going to be scared to come out in the yard. So, it's only right that you help us and handle it," he said.

At that moment, I remembered the words that Old Man Joe had told me about doing my time and no one else's.

"Well, like we said those that we are associated with would appreciate it very much."

"It's not my shit. I don't think I want to be involved," I said, as I got up and started to walk away.

"Hey youngster!" The guy in the muscle shirt yelled.

I turned to face him. At the time, I felt like I really didn't have the option not to.

"Think about it," he said. "It would be a shame if you were to be associated as one with Smiley. It would be a total shame."

I nodded my head as if I understood. Nervous and confused, I walked away from them as quick as I could. None of this was making any sense. *What the fuck did they want from me? I was just Smiley's cellmate.*

I walked into the day room to get some composure. I really didn't want to go back to the cell because I didn't know what to say to Smiley. *Should I tell him what was going on? Should I keep it to myself and see how this thing played out? What if he was telling the truth? Who were these guys, anyway?* "Hey Fernando," a voice called out. I turned to see who was speaking to me. It ended up being a guy by the name of Spanky. Spanky was one of the older guys that I knew from County.

"What's up Spanky?" I said, as I walked over to him.

"Not much. I understand you have your hands full though," he said, with much empathy.

"Shit, I don't know what's going on."

"Look homie, you'd better listen to those guys. They're hooked up with heavy people."

"Yeah, but I'm not sure who is telling the truth. Besides, it's none of my business," I replied.

"Listen, if they want you to whack Smiley, you'd better consider it. You could end up in the same situation."

"Shit."

"Yeah, I know homes, it's a messed up situation, but you still have to deal with it," he said.

I walked back to my cell dazed and confused. I still didn't know what I was going to say or ask Smiley, but I had to go somewhere.

Like Smiley, I was scared. I didn't want to kill anybody. I just wanted to do my time. *What the fuck was I going to do?*

Turns out, I wasn't going to have to do anything. When I got back to the cell all of Smiley's stuff was gone. He had rolled it up. I found out later that Smiley had told the cops that two other inmates were threatening him. He fingered the two that were questioning me in the chow hall earlier. In order to protect Smiley, they had him transferred to another prison. I guess as it turned out, it was best for all of us. Then I realized that some of my stuff was missing too; a few cosmetics, my picture of Vina, and my address book. All I could think was, *Smiley, that fucking piece of shit!* He turned out to be the rat that he was accused of after all.

CHAPTER 12

All prisons are overcrowded. This is one fact that prisoners, politicians, judges, and cops can all agree on. It is one of the reasons why riots start and one of the main reasons why some inmates are set free before their release date. Needless to say, I didn't have my own cell for any length of time. In only a matter of days, I got another cellmate. His name was Hoss.

Hoss was a lot older than me. His appearance was short and stocky, with no tattoos. To make him seem even more intimidating, he had lost his left eye in a prison knife fight years ago. A badass motherfucker from the word go—we clicked immediately.

"Are you going to be okay on the top bunk?" I asked.

"Yes, I'll be fine homie. I'm not that old yet, but thanks for asking," he replied.

"I didn't mean it like that, I, I just thought—"

"I know what you meant," he said, interrupting me. "Forget about it."

Nothing was said for the next few minutes as he unpacked his belongings. I finally broke the silence, but more than anything, I wished I hadn't. "So, tell me Hoss, what are you in here for?" I asked. At first he turned to me with a mad-dog stare, but then the tension in his face quickly melted away. I guess he came to the understanding that I wanted to make friends and small talk was the way I was going to make it happen. He also came to the understanding that I still was uneducated to the many ways of prison life.

So, instead of shunning my question, he used it as an opportunity to school me further about prison rules and etiquette.

"Well youngster, it's not polite to ask anyone about that, unless they share it with you."

Damn, I was embarrassed. More than anything I wanted to take the question back.

"Oh, I didn't know. I'm sorry, If I..." I said, as I fumbled for the correct words.

To save me from further embarrassment, he interrupted me.

"It's cool homie. Just remember what I told you for the next time." He smirked at me. "Well, I guess it's okay to tell you my claim to fame," he said. "I got twenty-five to life for the murder of my stepfather. He beat my mother one too many times. I just couldn't take it anymore. I was nineteen when it happened. Shit, now when I think about it, I've been in this hell-hole almost twenty years."

"Damn. Twenty years. Shit, I don't know what to say. I'm sorry man," I replied.

"It's cool homie. I've learned to deal with it. Just remember though, there are some guys who are not that comfortable, so be careful what you ask," he said.

That was the first lesson that Hoss had taught me. It was one of many.

The second major lesson that Hoss taught me was to have respect for the correctional officers. The concept behind this thought was that we were all stuck in here, so we should do our best to all get along. The more respect I showed to them, the more they would show to me and vice versa. Basically, prisoners wanted the most leniencies they could get to go with their jail terms, and in turn, the guards wanted to walk out of this prison on a daily basis—alive. Therefore, in most instances you found this underlying theme of mutual respect. This wasn't always the case though. Sometimes you would have a rookie cop who felt superior to everything and everyone. Those assholes often threw punches when they shouldn't have been thrown and they would sling shit where it shouldn't have been slung. Often, it would take a prison riot or one of them getting stabbed until they truly understood the rules of the game.

Likewise, you had young inmates that had the "fuck the police" attitude. They in turn, would have to get their ass beat by a half a dozen cops to figure out that they were not a force to mess with. Like Hoss told me, we were all on the same coin—one of us was heads, the other tails.

He was like my big brother and he often made me look at what I was going through in a different light. He shared his experiences with me in order to teach me how I should survive. He told me about being incarcerated within the system during the 1970's; when drugs almost doubled the amount that they were today, where everyone and their cellmate was strung out on some kind of drug or another. He spoke from experience as his drug of choice was heroin. He showed me the scars on his arms; permanent disfigurement from slamming a needle into his arm on a daily basis.

Time rolled on. Days turned into nights. Nights turned into days. I kept to myself most of the time, but every night Hoss and I would play our usual chess matches.

"I'll get the chess board," he said. "But first I need to take a piss. I'll meet you at the dayroom table."

Hoss and I were getting set up to play our daily chess match.

"Okay, cool. Let me just make my phone call real quick," I said.

It had been a few days since I called home. I missed my family terribly. When I walked into the area where the phones were, I noticed a black guy using the neutral phone. I just motioned to him that I was next. He sort of acknowledged my existence, but

I could tell that he was one of those "stress monsters"; always on the phone, wondering when "she" was going to visit, asking when "she" was going to bring him his shit, and constantly telling her that he loved her. Time was up; I motioned to him pointing at my wrist. He turned his back to me as if I wasn't even there. I tried to keep my cool and wait a few more minutes.

I thought he would have the common sense to get off the phone by himself without any altercation, but that wasn't about to be the case. After about three more minutes, I had enough.

"That's it man. It's my phone time," I said.

"I know man. Chill. Give me a second to hang up," he yelled, causing a scene.

It was like I was having a déjà vu moment. It reminded me so clearly of the problems that the Border Brother had in County, when he was trying to use the phones. He had been dishonored and disrespected by that Black guy, and even though he was in a totally different weight class, he still stood up for himself. In that moment, I was starting to get the inclination that I would have to do the same.

"Fuck that shit!" I yelled even louder, making an even bigger scene. "Give it up now."

Before I knew it, Hoss had grabbed me by my arm and was hauling me to the other side of the building.

"Relax homie," he said, both of us still moving in the opposite direction. "That's not how you deal with scum like that."

"Fuck that. What about my phone call?" I said.

"Forget it. We'll deal with that shit later. C'mon."

"That's some Bullshit man, he fucked me out of my phone call."

"Relax man," Hoss said, through gritted teeth.

Before I knew it he grabbed my arm again and was hustling

me even further from the situation. Within a couple of seconds we were both outside.

"Cool down youngster," Hoss said.

"Hoss, you don't understand."

"I do understand. Look homie, if you would've continued yelling, the C.O. would have seen you guys and turned off the phones for everybody. Then everybody would have taken it out on both of you," he said. "Just relax and let a few days go by. Cool off and *then* we'll get the bastard."

I don't know how he did it, but Hoss cooled me down. I would take his advice and let it be. As a matter of fact, for the next few days I continued to listen to Hoss and I acted like nothing ever happened. Believe me, it was one of the hardest things I ever did. I noticed that the Black guy would smirk every time he would see me. *That bastard.* I wanted to take flight on sight, but I just ignored him like Hoss told me to. Hoss had a better plan.

"Tie it up real tight and don't forget to wrap it up good in your jacket pocket and get rid of it soon after." Hoss had showed me how to make a weapon out of a bar of soap and a D battery. He had me put both in a tube sock and tied the end several times so that it would act as a good handle. Around the tip of the sock where the soap and the battery lay, we wrapped tape so that it wouldn't break.

"So, run it by me again Hoss. How are we going to do this shit?" I said.

"Well, like I said, we're going to try to make it happen during shift change. The C.O.'s are usually busy trying to rush in and out of here and they usually aren't aware of everyone just yet. That should give you a few seconds to do your deal," he said.

He paused for a minute. I guess it was to see if I was paying attention or to look into my eyes to evaluate if I was up to the task.

"Now remember, first walk around the day room till you're

away from everyone. Then wait till I give you the signal and walk up behind him and pound his head as he talks away on the phone. I'll be your look out and I will yell out to you when to stop so you could get a quick getaway. Now remember, don't stop pounding until you hear my voice, but once I tell you to stop, you stop. This is not debatable. Put the sock calmly back in your waist and walk away. Walk away as if you don't even know who the fuck did it. Get it?"

"Yeah Hoss, I got it," I replied.

For a couple hours, Hoss and I waited in our cell for the unlock. To Hoss, it probably seemed as no big deal, but to me it felt like I had already served my prison term within those few hours. If I listened hard enough, I could hear every click of the clock.

Then it happened. All at once the cells unlocked and everybody headed out into the dayroom, including Hoss and I. "Now, stop when I say stop," Hoss reiterated. On the outside, I walked confident and with a purpose. On the inside, I was a nervous wreck. I was worried about getting caught by the C.O.'s or worse yet, getting shot by the gunner. Inside of my prison blues my body was sweating profusely. Part of me wanted to call it off, but I took a deep breath and continued on my mission. When I got to the day room, I noticed that he wasn't on the phone yet so I just sat by the TV, alone, waiting for that son of a bitch to make his move.

Sure enough, it happened. He went over to the drinking fountain and I got the nod from Hoss. I knew that if I didn't get him now, I wouldn't have a chance the next time around. *BAM! BAM!* I hit him twice in the head. Everyone else scattered as if they were going to be next. To my surprise, when I turned back to the Black guy was out cold. I didn't think I would actually do it with two blows, but I had accomplished my mission. Like Hoss had taught me, I started to tuck the sock in my waist band, but it was too late. Before I knew it a loud buzzer was going off.

"Get down!" the C.O. yelled, as he cocked back on his mini-14. He was ready to blow a hole right through the center of me and the look on his face told me that he was more than determined to do so. I lay on the floor slowly, but as I did so I looked over to Hoss. I thought he would be upset that I was caught, but to my surprise the look on his face was more of approval. Of course he was disappointed that I had been caught, but I had accomplished what I had set out to do—I had set out to get some respect. I was escorted to medical, for evaluation then sent to my new housing location, "The Hole".

CHAPTER 13

They put me in a one man cell; a phone booth size cage. Boxer shorts and handcuffs were all I had on. I stood there alone until they brought in a few more inmates from other facilities. I was joined by three young Blacks and one older White guy—each in their own one man cell. The White guy was celled right next to me. I noticed he took a knee and started praying as soon as his cuffs came off.

Being so close to me, I could actually hear what he was whispering. Then before I could drift away from his rubbish, I heard him mentioning me. "Yes Lord, I ask you to touch this man's heart next to me, Father, and I pray you go before him in front of the judgment coming upon him to allow a fair outcome, Lord. In Jesus' name, amen." He stood up, looked directly at me, and I at him. "ROCHA!" yelled the C.O. walking up to my cell. I turned to face him. "Turn around, need to uncuff you, we're taking you to your housing." As I turned around and stuck my hands through a slot, the White guy whispered to me. "Jeremiah 33:3," he said. I knew he was mentioning a bible verse, and I just nodded my head. As I was being escorted down the corridor to my cell, I was thinking about the White guy's prayer, and the Bible verse. "Jeremiah 33:3, Jeremiah 33:3," I kept repeating till I just about memorized the scripture.

The guy that they locked me up with was a Mexican who didn't speak English. As a matter of fact, he really didn't speak much at all. If he did communicate, it mostly came out as a mouthful of gibberish. It didn't take me long to figure out that he was mentally disturbed. So, there I was, holed up with this dingbat. After spending a couple of days with him, I started to notice that this dude was really messed up in the head. When he did talk to me, what I did start to understand was that he was into devil worship. If he wasn't expressing his ideas on the Prince of Darkness, he was usually talking to himself. Upon closer observation, I noticed that he had self-inflicted tattoos. Scar tissue stuck out from parts of his shoulders and arms; some of the images recognizable as the number six. Others were not as clear, but I guess that is what you get when you're trying to create a lot of detail with a knife. I had done some stupid things in my life and I was about to do some more, but you would never catch me carving an image into my body with a blade.

After awhile they gave me my sneakers back and I got to wear a brand spanking new red jumpsuit. We also got two hours of yard once a week. Let me tell you, that was the highlight of my stay there. For a hundred and twenty minutes out of the week, I got a chance to pace back and forth inside an eight by eight cage. Shit, I could probably stretch my arms wide enough to touch both ends. It felt like a dog kennel for humans. On the other hand, I got to breathe fresh air. So there we were, my cellmate and I, both of us pacing back and forth, doing nothing, saying nothing—just breathing.

There was a toilet and shower in the cage. I didn't have to guess what the temperature of the water would be—damn near freezing. The boredom was constantly with me; this dingbat cellmate wasn't helping. The most I could do was read during the day. The C.O.'s passed by once or twice a week with a cart full of books. As an inmate in the hole, you didn't get a chance to browse the selections and pick up a subject of interest. You kind of had to grab one or two books that looked interesting as the cart continued to roll by. Once a week, I got enough paper, a small pencil, and an envelope with one stamp in order to write a letter to family. Even though they couldn't immediately reply back, I made them my company as I did my time in the hole.

One morning I was escorted out of my cell to the L.T.'s office for my hearing. It was a basic formality that lets you know why you're in the hole, charges against you, and how you plea. I was put into a one man cage again whilst the L.T. stood in front, questioning me. "Mr. Rocha, you are being charged with assault and battery on inmate Johnson." He went on with more hogwash about the incident, but honestly, I was spaced out in thought. Finally, he began to talk normal. "Okay, Rocha. Here's the thing, you *Vatos Locos* and the Brother's have been a pain in my fat ass!" He removed his shades to wipe his face of sweat. "I interviewed inmate Johnson and he's not talking and doesn't want to identify you as the suspect, HOWEVER! Mr. Rocha, we know you did this shit. My gunner knows you did this shit. So, let's cut the bullshit paper work, get you to plead guilty, will give you a one year suspended security housing. Look, you'll do a few more months in the hole, then kick you back out to a main line, what do you say?" he said, as he handed me the pen. I signed, and was escorted back to my cell.

The C.O. uncuffed me and my cell door opened. This nasty shit odor came upon me as I walked in my cell. "WHAT THE FUCK!" I began to instantly gag. I covered my mouth and nose, looked at my cellmate thinking he passed gas, but to my surprise there was a huge piece of shit right on the desk, of all places.

"What the fuck is wrong with you!" I yelled.

He stood up, screaming, "*SATANAS!*" (Lucifer) then rushed me!

I front kicked him and he fell back to the bottom bunk. When he tried to rush me again, I somehow maneuvered him up against the cell door. All my aggression, all my frustration, and all of my anger, I let off on this guy. Before I knew it, the cell door was open;

tear gas was all I could inhale. Finally, we were dragged out the cell and sent to medical. Same formality as before, but this time I was met there by the L.T. who'd just interviewed me. "WHAT THE FUCK, ROCHA!" he yelled. I couldn't quite see from the tear gas yet, but I recognized the voice. The L.T. had them shower me off and began his questioning. There was no getting around it and the truth is, it's what actually spared me more hole time. The L.T. reviewed my cellmate's case file and confirmed he was a 5150 (mentally disturbed). Technically, he was not supposed to be housed with general population inmates. He was to be housed in the medical ward. The L.T. took that into consideration, didn't charge me, and housed me in a new cell.

This time, I had no cellmate. The whole tier was full of one man cells. I did see the other inmates on my tier at yard—each in our own kennel. After a few months alone, I started to have some type of anxiety. I read all the books, some twice, and you could only workout, jack-off, so much. I started talking to myself. I even invented a game to keep my mind occupied. I'd save my diced carrots from dinner and then allow them to dry up till they were hard as wood. I'd grab however many I had, stand at the cell door with my back to my cell, and I'd toss the carrots behind me, till they scattered everywhere. Then I would close my eyes, turn around, and just with my hands look for them till I found each one. Sometimes it took 10 minutes and other days took hours.

I avoided the huge King James Bible that would always travel along the selection cart. I'm not sure what moved me to grab it that day, but I did, and got a funny look from the C.O. I tossed it on my bunk and stood at the cell door staring out into the building. I noticed the older White guy, who was praying next to my one man cell before. It looked as though he was being escorted out with other inmates. As he stood in line, he looked up directly at me. I focused on his face; he nodded, then looked straight up, smiled, and was escorted away. That was the creepiest shit ever.

At that moment, I remembered "Jeremiah 33:3" and looked it up. I tried to read the Bible once in juvie-camp, but I couldn't understand it. I found the scripture, Jeremiah-33:3, it read: "Call unto me, and I will answer thee, and show the great and mighty things, which thou knowest not." I read it a few times, and set the Bible down. I started to wonder if encountering this older White dude was like a sign from God or something. After spending six and a half months in that hell-hole, I was called back to the L.T.'s office for an evaluation.

"So Mr. Rocha, how's everything going with you?" he smirked, as he leaned over his desk.

"Never better L.T.," I replied. I was beat to shit, but I wouldn't let him know it.

"Well, being that your security points have gone up, and it's close to your annual review, we're transferring you to a higher level security prison," he said.

"What prison would I be put up for?" I asked.

He stood up and waved the escorting officer in to take me back to my cell. "There are two options right now, CSP-Corcoran or our level four yard next door. Sacramento Prison Board will determine the outcome. It will take a few days, or weeks. Hang tight, Rocha, and stay out of trouble."

"Hell, what kind of trouble can I possibly get into in a one man cell, L.T.?"

The L.T. just smirked as the escorting officer grabbed my arm and walked me back to my cell.

After a few days, I was awoken at 3:00 a.m. by my cell door opening. I jumped on my feet for some reason and stood in fight stance. "Stand down, Rocha, roll your shit up, you're transferring!"

the C.O. said. He slammed my cell door. "I'll be back for you in 10 minutes, feed the sharks (take a shit) now, because we have a long bus ride." I didn't have much, so I actually was ready to go, but I took his advice and fed the sharks. My nerves started fucking with me. As I washed my hands I could hear that officer walking back towards my cell. My cell door opened. "Step out, hands against the wall." He patted me down, for some reason, and cuffed me. We headed out to Receiving and Release. Then, I'm put back into that one man cell.

"Getting the paper work in order, Rocha, and we're outta here!" he said, as he locked the cell.

"Where are we headed to C.O.?" I asked.

"Next stop, Corcoran State Prison!" he yelled out.

CHAPTER 14

B uilt on 940 acres of cotton country in the San Joaquin Valley, Corcoran State Prison was home to Charles Manson, Sirhan Sirhan, and other notorious criminals. It earned a reputation as a repository for the worst of the worst. The ironic thing is, it was a fairly new prison. Next to Pelican Bay, a prison on the far North Coast of California that's been around much longer, Corcoran is one of, if not the most notorious prison to date.

We arrived at nighttime. Huge stadium lighting illuminated the yard. It looked to be at least a hundred inmates walking around in there. It was cold that evening. I shivered under my jumpsuit; a mist of my breath evaporated into the dark cloudless night. I had heard many brutal and heartless stories of things that had happened in Corcoran, but none were wilder than what I was about to encounter. No sign of emotion came across my face. No fear in my body language. I was ready to face this prison time head on. The experience in county and the advice I was given, has prepared me for what's to come.

The group that I was chained to was all headed for security level 4. You don't get placed in a security level 4 unless you have a high risk security level. Since I popped that guy in Tehachapi and being transferred from the hole, I was considered a candidate. We were quickly escorted to a holding tank in order to be processed. It was a cage—a square box about ten by ten made of chain link fence. There we were given a lime green jumpsuit that we were told to quickly change into.

Actually, it really wasn't too bad inside the cage. There was a toilet in there, a TV with CNN on it, and they gave us a sack lunch which consisted of a cheese sandwich, an apple, and a couple of graham crackers. The only problem was the cheese sandwich was thick, hard, and had the odor of funky feet, the apple was mushy like baby food, and the graham crackers were just plain stale. I ate anyway. I was hungry and I had no idea when my next meal was coming.

"Rez, Williams, Garcia, Rocha," a voice boomed. I jumped up. "Single file hands behind your back," one of the C.O.'s yelled. We were greeted by four of them as one of them unlocked the cage. I was the last one in line. "Follow us." Surrounded by the four C.O.'s, we walked out of the cage. "Hold it up. Hold it up," the first C.O. bellowed. He acted like he was a traffic cop and the presidential motorcade was cruising by. Nevertheless, we all stopped dead in our tracks right in front of a white door. "Clear yard for transfer. Clear yard for transfer," he barked into the transmitter of a two-way radio. "Clear the yard for escort. Clear the yard for escort," a voice boomed outside the door on a loud speaker. "Clear the yard for transfer." Immediately, the first C.O. opened the door and we were escorted into the yard. In the same instance, the inmates in the yard started to separate, leaving us an aisle way to walk straight through. Like Moses parting the Red Sea, some inmates went left, others wound up on our right side, but no one stood closer than twenty feet away.

We came to a place that I assumed was another laundry room. It was a clean place, full of whites, and it smelled good. Towards the back, behind a mesh screen, inmates were handing out clothes. We were given a little piece of paper and a small pencil in order to mark our sizes. Back then I always wore clothes that were too big for me. It was the style. Normally my pants size would be a thirty-two waist, so I marked down size forty. I wore a medium to a large shirt, but I made sure to order a 2X-large. Handing the slip of paper to the C.O. he rolled his eyes and read off the sizes, "This guy will take a size thirty pants and a medium shirt."

This was messed up. Now my clothes were going to be too tight. Shit, I was going to be walking around here like Pee-Wee Herman. I guess since I put some outrageous sizes, the C.O. took it upon himself to be my personal tailor. I was handed a blue state shirt and blue state pants. Then I was handed my boots, a size ten— my correct size. To my surprise the boots that they issued us were nice. They were almost something that I would wear on the outside. They were dark brown, made of leather, and had quite a nice style to them. After putting on my state blues, I slipped them on. "Tuck in your shirt," one of the C.O.'s yelled.

Once everyone was dressed into their new outfits, they once again cleared the yard for escort. This time, instead of walking through the center of the yard, we walked around the perimeter. Stopping at every building, the first C.O. examined his clipboard to see if someone was to be dropped off there. The first two guys were placed in building four and the third guy was dropped off at building two. I however, was placed in building one which mostly housed lifers. We came to the entrance of building one, the focal point of my stay here at Corcoran.

It was a large building, with two tiers, built in the shape of a horseshoe. As I entered, I practically stood underneath the control tower and looked over my future home. There were four staircases and each one was placed in a corner, leading up to the second tier. It was massive in size and I couldn't help but think of how many of us were in here. This was just one building out of one yard. Corcoran State Prison had five yards with each yard having five buildings.

Within minutes, I was approached by the C.O. who I guessed was in charge for the evening. Actually, he acted, looked, and talked as if he wanted to play warden. He was a short Asian guy that looked like he spent all of his spare time working out in the gym. Not only was he flushed with arrogance, he had a body that was as short as it was wide, which gave him the biggest Napoleon complex ever.

"So, we've got a prize-fighter here," he said aloud, as he read my card.

My card was basically a rap sheet of my prison time, and why I was there.

"So, are we going to have a problem with our prize-fighter?" he asked after he finished reading my card.

I shook my head. "Not at all boss," I mumbled.

I was led up to the second tier. Each cell had a door with a rectangular window of unbreakable glass in it. Controlled by the gun tower, each door was operated by a noisy locking system that could open one cell at a time or all of them together. At this particular time it only opened up mine. It was in cell number 216 that I met Chico, a short, lanky, Hispanic, lifer.

"What's up," I said in a cool, impersonal tone, as I walked in and put my stuff down.

"What's up," he replied. "You'll have to take the top bunk homes," he motioned with a nod of his head.

I placed the few belongings I had on the top bunk and then decided that it would be appropriate to introduce myself.

"I'm Fernando," I said.

"I'm Chico," he replied. He didn't even really look up.

The cell was rather barren. Chico had no pictures hanging on the wall and only one small paperback book lay on the shelf next to the bunk. Unlike some of the cells that had all the amenities of home, TV, radio, throw rug, food, or cosmetics, this place had really nothing. I could only guess that Chico had just arrived here also.

"I just got out of Tehachapi," I said, trying to strike up some kind of conversation. "I was just in the hole."

"Really?" he said.

I shook my head as if I had accomplished something admirable and Chico was giving me recognition for my achievement.

"Damn, that's not a hole." Chico smirked. "I could do at least a year standing on my head in there."

For a second I felt frozen, a bit dumbfounded. I had just lived through the hardest six months of my life and this asshole was down playing it like it was just a walk in the park. There are probably a couple thousand inmates here and I had to get celled up with this motherfucker.

"You want to see a hole?" he asked, motioning me towards the window. "Now that's a fuckin' hole," he said, pointing out the window.

I went to the window to take a peak.

"Look to the west."

"That big gray building over there?" I asked.

"That's the one, Corcoran's Security Housing Unit. It's on and cracking there. They have guards setting up fights between races. Real dirt-bag shit these C.O.'s are pulling, lots of inmates getting stabbed and then shot by the active gunner. They just smoked this Black fool while he was defending himself from two Skin Heads trying to kill him. Racist cops are going to get theirs real soon," he continued to say, while I looked out the window.

It stood about fifty yards away and even though I knew it was different, it looked exactly the same as the place that we were locked under.

"Corcoran S.H.U., otherwise known as Gladiator School," Chico went on to say.

"No shit," I said.

"Well listen youngster, I'm going to step out for awhile, let you get situated. Help yourself to anything you need."

I looked at his shelf locker—it was practically empty. I looked back at him, he laughed, turned on his heels, and walked out into the yard.

CHAPTER 15

U nexpectedly, I found a razor, deodorant, toothbrush, tooth-paste, and a bar of soap on the shelf near my head when I woke up the next morning. As I looked over to him, he was totally dressed, boots on, ready to go.

"You going to breakfast?" Chico barked.

"Fuck yea," I replied.

"They're going to pop the cell in ten minutes. You have time to get ready."

Chico sat on the desk while I washed up and dressed for chow. He stared out the window, looking toward the SHU. "Some shit is going down today next door."

I spit toothpaste into the toilet and responded. "Is that right?"

"I was talking to my homeboy on the yard last night, word is they're going at it hard with the Blacks," Chico said.

I was tying my shoes when the cell door opened.

Chico stood up. "Hold on youngster, let me put you up on something."

I stood up facing him, still in our cell.

"Be on your toes at all times, there's a lot of tension right now because of what's happening next door. No telling how soon this prison is going to erupt," he said.

I nodded that I understood.

"Hey Chico, thanks for the cosmetics," I said, as we sat down to eat our breakfast.

"Ah, don't sweat it youngster. I keep all my stuff in boxes under the bunk. It's an old habit I have," he said.

I noticed most of the Blacks had on like two jackets and the White guys were talking very secretive amongst themselves. You could definitely feel some tension. Chico began asking me questions.

"So, what they got you for youngster?"

I looked at him and I smirked. "Attempted murder," I replied.

"What you down for?"

"Ten years."

He looked puzzled. "Where did the person get hit or how badly injured?" he asked.

"No one actually got hit, just shot at."

He looked on disapproving. "Wait a minute!" He finished chewing his eggs before he continued. "You mean to tell me, you got ten years for attempted murder, and no one was hit?"

I started to analyze what he was saying and before I could answer, he burst out, "YOUNGSTER! You got railroaded! Your attorney is a piece of shit! He knew better then to convince you that you got a fair trial!"

I actually lost my appetite. It's obvious I was railroaded. What Chico was saying actually made sense.

"Damn, what can I do now, I already got sentenced," I said, as I took a sip of coffee.

"That don't mean shit," Chico said.

"But—" I didn't get a chance to respond before Chico interrupted me.

"See here, youngster." He put down his fork and stopped eating. "They railroaded your ass." He started to smirk. "What you need to do is file a motion to appeal your case." We got up to turn in our trays and he continued. "You have a lot of action at least getting your sentenced reduced. The charge of attempted murder doesn't apply to your case. No one was injured, how can it be an attempted murder? Makes no sense," he said.

"Damn, Chico, it sounds hopeful, but I don't have money for a lawyer," I said.

"Shit, you don't need a fucking lawyer. Start your own appeal," he said, as we walked into the yard from the mess hall. "Once the appeals court grants your motion then you can ask for a state appointed attorney. Those attorneys are better than the public defenders you had in L.A. County."

"Man, I don't know the first thing about the legal system," I said.

"And you think I was born with wisdom?" he snapped. "Look, you don't need to be a lawyer to file your paperwork, what are you going to do right now, youngster?"

"Well, I was thinking about going out in the yard. I was going to see if any of my homies were here."

"Shit, you got ten years to start your scandalous life in that yard. Do you want to start your appeal?"

"Of course I do," I quickly replied.

"Then fuck that yard shit for now. Come with me to the library."

I nodded. So, there I was a half an hour later, looking through shelves of law books without the faintest clue of what I was looking for.

"Here, you need these," Chico said, as he plopped several books into my arms. "Look man, I don't even do this for my own homeboys."

"Thanks for helping me, Chico," I said.

"Shit youngster, you're the one that's going to do the work. I'm just going to guide you. You're young, you've been fucked by the system, and you don't belong in this hell-hole. Maybe you even still have a chance. Hopefully, you'll get a few years knocked off your sentence," Chico said.

We spent most of our time at the law library, our heads buried in some type of law book or another, me fighting my case, and he fighting his. Other than what pertained to law, we spoke a bit about his case. I had come to understand that Chico was serving a life sentence for a murder he was convicted of in 1983. He was at least twenty years older than me, but the hard time he'd already served had aged him tremendously. If I had to guess, he could have been my father's age. Tattoos covered most of his body; symbols and pictures all telling of a rough youth and hardcore prison time. The scars from stab wounds acted as a memorial to all the crazy riots he had been in. Several contusions on his arms remained as little mementos from all the cop beatings he received while incarcerated. Over the past ten years, he had taught himself to be a jailhouse lawyer. With extensive reading and studying, he had acquired more knowledge about criminal law than an average public defender. As much as he studied the law however, he hated the system and used every opportunity to break it. He felt that if he could get himself out or anyone else out, then he was winning. It was his game in prison—his reason for waking up every day. It's why he held a job in the law library five days a week.

Through the weeks on, he continued to help with my appeal process and once all our motions were filed, there was nothing else to do but wait. I stopped going to the library every day and just popped my head in occasionally to mess with Chico. I would play handball every day after breakfast. After handball I would lift weights. Every evening after dinner, I would take a walk out into the yard. I did this by myself. I wanted to be alone. Alone in my thoughts, contemplating all the reasons why I was here, wondering what I was going to do with my life when I got out. I missed home

more than ever. What guys in prison call, hard timing. I continued
to shuffle towards several guys sitting at some tables in a corner of
the yard. From a distance I couldn't tell, but as I got closer I could
see that a chess match was taking place. For a moment, I had found
a distraction to jolt me out of the funk that I was in. I loved chess.
In fact, I was turning into a chess fanatic. I couldn't help but stop to
watch. As I got there, the old man's rook was about to be taken by
the younger guy's queen.

"Good move," I blurted out, as the young guy slid his queen
across the board. The young guy turned to look at me. He stared me
down, as if to say, "who asked you?"

"You fuck around, homie?" he said to me, as he sized me up
and down.

"Yeah, a little bit."

"Well, then you can have the next game," he said.

"Cool," I responded. Within a few more moves, the older guy
was checkmated.

"Well, that's enough ass-whipping for me today," the older guy
said. "I'll see you tomorrow, Spider."

"Okay Pops, I'll see you later," Spider replied. Then he
turned to me.

"So, Black or White?" he asked.

"Black," I responded.

To describe Spider would be to simply say his name. A tall,
skinny fool, that had tattoos covering most of his body, and he
sported one of those large mustaches. Spider was only a few years
older than me, but he was a lot wiser. This was his second term in
prison, so he had a lot of knowledge of prison ways. He and I became good friends from that day forward.

Later that night, Chico sparked up a conversation like if he'd
been drinking a bit too much coffee. He spoke about his family,

about his life before prison, and his hope to one day be a free man even though it was highly unlikely that the day would ever come. There was a few minutes pause then I broke the ice.

"Hey Chico, why are these C.O.'s different than the deputies in L.A. County Jail?"

"Well, these C.O.'s give us respect because in turn we give it to them. You see youngster, we are all doing a lot of time here. Most of us life. That doesn't mean we don't care anymore or feel that we should give up on living." He paused for a few seconds. "The C.O.'s, they are doing their time also," he said. "They do their time every stinking day from nine to five. Sure they go home from work, but some of them, I've often heard say, that they live happier in here than at home with their bitching wives." He smirked. "I'm not saying that the C.O.'s aren't assholes. A lot of them are racist pigs." Then he paused, contemplated, and reflected. "Then again, we've gone to war with them several times in the past, and I'm sure we will go again sometime in the future."

"So Chico, since there are so many of us in here, are we the strongest?" I asked.

"We are a strong group," he replied.

"So, what you are saying is that the Hispanics are one of the most dangerous in this prison," I replied.

"No youngster. Neither are the Blacks or the Whites."

"Well then, who controls the prison system?" I asked.

Chico started to laugh. *Did I say something stupid?* Then as quickly as he started to laugh, he once again became serious.

"Hate. Hate is in control of the prison. It controls all the ignorant and the weak and it is our ignorance and weakness that controls us."

"So what you're saying is that we all are in control of the prison, but it's the hate that is in control of us?" I said.

"That's right youngster. You see the Whites got their thing, they call it "White Pride", the Blacks got the muscle, and the Mexicans got the knives. As one we have all of that. Together we are strong, but apart we are just hate. Color separates all of us," Chico said. With that Chico got up to pick his face in the mirror.

"Hey Chico, you know what I'd really like to do?"

"What's that youngster?" Chico asked as he washed his hands.

"I'd like to go to school."

He laughed again. "Shit youngster, you'll be two months sitting at home before you get a *ducat* to go to school here. Do you know how long the waiting list is to get in? Shit, you'd better stick to looking for a kitchen job."

With that, lights out.

CHAPTER 16

Several days later, I woke up, rolled over, and there was a *ducat* on the shelf locker. In prison, a *ducat* is a little slip of paper that is given to you by an automated system that assigns jobs, school, and any other type of movement within the facility. Once you get this ducat it is mandatory that you show up at school or the job you were commissioned to. I was assigned to a.m. kitchen duty. I didn't start till Monday morning which gave me a couple days. I washed up, and minutes later, cell was open for chow. As I strolled into the mess hall, I noticed Spider and I caught up with him.

"What's up Spider?" I said, all excited, ready to show off my ducat.

"Not much, Fernando," he said, in a rather solemn voice. "What's up with you?"

I could tell he was stressing about something. If anything could be said about Spider, he always had a pretty positive attitude.

"What's on your mind, homie?" I asked.

We went through the breakfast line in silence. We got our eggs, toast, and coffee. It was business as usual, but one look in Spider's eyes told me that something was not right. I followed Spider as he walked with his tray. He sat as far away from everybody else as he could. Deliberately and slowly he looked around before he began speaking.

"Dog, check it out, I got a note from this guy that just got out of the hole yesterday. It came down from a made guy, one of my older homies."

"Oh shit, what did it say?" I asked.

"Well it turns out that one of my homeboys from my neighborhood, this guy named Stranger, got busted for some drive-by shooting that resulted in a young girl's death."

"Yeah, what's the big deal? People die all the time in drive-bys," I said.

"Well that young girl that was killed, her pops is from the mob."

"Oh shit! I said.

"Basically, they are going to want him dead. The problem is that if he comes to this yard, they want me to handle him."

I frowned trying to think of something to say. "Don't trip man. What are the chances of him coming here?"

"I don't know," Spider replied.

"Don't trip, Spider. Deal with it when it happens."

After breakfast, we headed out into the yard. I could tell this was weighing heavily on Spider's mind. I figured this would be a good time to tell him the news. Maybe distract him from stressing.

"Spider, I got a kitchen job," I said.

"That's good homie, when do you start?"

"Monday," I said.

"Man, you going to be eating good as a motherfucker," Spider said, as he rubbed his stomach.

We walked the track a few laps then Spider began heading back to his cell. "I'm going to make a few calls dog. I'll see ya later," Spider said, as he fist bumped me.

"Alright homie, catch you later," I replied.

I went to the library. I saw Chico sitting at a table.

"Sup cellie?" I said.

He looked up at me, nodded his head, and continued to thumbed through a huge law book. I left him alone and wondered into the class room areas. Walking down the corridor I noticed this older

Black man writing math problems on the board. He must have sensed that I was looking because he stopped writing, then turned around, saw me, but I turned and walked away. As I was leaving the library, Chico stopped me.

"Hey, cellie, hold up."

"What's going on Chico?" I asked.

"I heard about Spider's homeboy, Stranger."

I looked both ways and responded. "It's some fucked up shit."

We started walking towards our cell block.

"Yeah, I know, I heard all about it," he said.

Chico is up to date with everything on the yard. All the prison time he's served has definitely kept him in the know. As we got to our cell block, he continued to speak.

"Man, the day that girl got killed, homies from Spider's neighborhood were acting squirrelly."

Walking into our cell-block we stopped talking till we reached our cell door.

"Do you think he should be dealt with?" I asked, just as we walked into our cell. I began to wash my hands as he put his folders away.

"Look, I know if the father of the girl wasn't affiliated, it wouldn't be like this," Chico said.

Drying my hands I turned to face him.

"It's politics," he said.

The weekend passed.

Finally, it was Monday morning. I just finished rinsing off my toothbrush. My cell door opened at 5:00 a.m. and the cell block officer yelled out, "Kitchen workers, head out!" I finished getting dressed and headed out. I noticed a group of cooks already at the grills. I walked over to the officer on duty, *MS. SANDOVAL.* She

was a newbie officer, at least in her early twenty's. I approached
from behind as she was talking to a couple other guys with ducats.

"Make sure you respect my kitchen, and if I catch you stealing,
I will directly escort you to the security housing unit, we understood?" she said.

The guys nodded. "Understood."

They grabbed some cleaning rags and wiped the mess hall tables. She turned around and faced me. "Who are you?" she said
with attitude. I gave her my ducat. "Mr. Rocha, okay, let's see what
we can assign you." We walked to her office which is in the middle
of the kitchen and the serving area. I noticed a White inmate clerk
sitting at a desk next to hers. She grabbed a clip board and wrote
my information on it. "Okay, I got you on pots and pans scullery,"
she said, and motioned for me to follow her. We got to the dish
washing area and she pointed out what would be my station for the
next few hours. I saw the huge pile of trays and pans.

"Oh shit!" I whispered.

"Oh shit is right, get to it." she smiled, and walked away.

I couldn't help notice how beautiful she was. She looked very
fit, too.

After work, I was beat. I wanted to hit the showers and take a
long nap. Walking towards my cell block I saw Spider sitting at a
table watching the handball games. I made my way towards him.
Being able to work in the kitchen, you're allowed some perks, as long
as the officer is aware. I took a couple bags of grilled cheese sand-
wiches and ice cold juices. Spider saw me walking up and stood up.

"Sup dog," he said, and fist bumped me. "Whatcha got there,
big homie?" he said, with a big Kool-Aid simile.

I handed him a bag. "Here you go, that's for you."

He grabbed it and immediately opened it. "Fuck yeah, I love
grill cheese." He took a bite and smiled. "*Gracias*, homie."

"I'm going to head in, shower, and chill for a bit, catch you later, dog," I said, as I was about to head out.

"Clear yard for transfer. Clear yard for transfer," a voice boomed over the loudspeaker. With that everything stopped, as a group of new men were being led through the center of the yard. "Fernando, come here," Spider said quietly, as he walked to the edge of the court. I quickly fell into step and I was right behind him. He shook his head in the direction that he wanted me to look. "That's my homeboy Stranger," he said. Together we watched the procession of the six new prisoners as they each were put in their respective new homes. "Shit, I hope they don't put him in my building," Spider said, in a barely audible whisper.

As luck would have it, Stranger was escorted to building one. The same building that Spider and I were housed in. Spider and I made our way towards our building. Spider wanted to talk to Stranger and asked if I would come with him.

"No problem," I replied.

"Thanks dog."

"Look Spider, don't worry. No matter what happens, I'll be there, no matter what you decide to do. I got your back," I said.

"Thanks Fernando. That means a lot to me."

As we got closer to the building, two guys approached Spider.

"Spider, make sure he's is dealt with ASAP," the first guy remarked.

I recognized the guy who spoke as one of the guys who ran the yard. He was entangled with the mob which in turn made him a person not to be fucked with.

"Yeah, I know what's up," Spider retorted. "Don't trip, I'll take care of it."

It was obvious that Spider was clearly annoyed at the situation and angry at all the pressure he was being put under. I really couldn't blame him.

As we reached Stranger's cell, I was a bit taken aback at what I saw. I really didn't get a good look at Stranger while in the yard, but I perceived him to be a bit of a tough motherfucker. When I looked at him up close, I was staring at someone that looked younger than me. *Shit, he looked like a kid.* I could barely believe that he just turned eighteen. I don't think he was even into shaving yet, which made him appear even younger.

"Hey homeboy, what's up? I heard you were here," Spider said, as he saw Stranger.

Stranger immediately jumped up and embraced Spider. "What's up Spider? My older brother said you were here."

"That's right," Spider replied. "How is that fool?"

"He's alright. You know how it is. Every day is a struggle, but he's just trying to do his own thing," Stranger said.

"That's right," Spider said, as he nodded his head and searched for something else to say. "Hey, homes, this is my roll-dog, Fernando from West L.A."

"Hey, what's up Stranger," I said, as I extended my hand. "How you doing? Do you need anything? Cosmetics, food, anything?" I tried to show him the same hospitality that I had been shown when I first arrived in County so many months ago.

There was a contract out on Stranger's life, but it still didn't mean that he shouldn't be treated with respect by a fellow Hispanic brother. It wasn't as if he was a rat or something like that. He had just made a grave mistake like all of us have at one time or another.

"No thanks man. I'm okay," Stranger replied. "Most of my stuff is pretty stocked up."

"Well listen homie, unpack your stuff, relax, and join us out in the yard tomorrow," Spider said. "We'll talk a bit then."

"That's cool Spider. I'd like that. It's good that you found me, I got some stuff I need to talk to you about too," Stranger said.

With that Spider and I both left for our respective cells. Chico was already there, sitting facing out the back window. As I closed the cell door behind me, he turned to face me.

"Are you going to help him whack Stranger?"

It was obvious he knew Stranger was here already. I set my things down, and then responded.

"Yes, if he needs my help."

Chico nodded his head.

As tired as I was, I didn't sleep a wink that night and I doubt that Spider did either. Stranger seemed like a cool guy. He had just fucked up. There had to be a better solution to this problem. Chico noticed I couldn't sleep.

"You still thinking about Stranger, cellie?"

I jumped off my bunk and walked up to the cell door. Staring out the window toward Stranger's cell. I turned to face Chico. "Is there a way for Stranger to get out of this?"

Chico stood up and leaned up against the wall. "No, not really," he said. "I don't think something like this can be cleaned up, you know?"

I nodded in agreement.

"However, it's worth a shot," Chico said.

I jumped back into bed and tried to sleep.

Then next morning at work, I stepped out the dishwashing area, and I noticed Spider and Stranger eating breakfast. Spider saw me and motioned he'd wait for me to get off at the same table. I raised a thumbs up.

"Rocha!" yelled Ms. Sandoval. "Why aren't you at your station?"

I was caught by surprise. "Oh, my bad Ms. Sandoval," I said, as I hurried back to my station.

"What are you doing away from your assigned work area, anyway?"

She walked me all the way back.

I continued washing pots and said, "Sorry about that Ms. Sandoval, was looking for a friend of mine, guy I grew up with, I heard he arrived yesterday."

She rolled her eyes and walked away.

I finally finished my shift and I was heading out. I noticed Ms. Sandoval was searching everyone more than usual. She went from a light pat down to checking every pocket and emptying everyone's "goodie" bags. My turn came up.

"Empty out all your bags, and hands against the wall," she ordered. I did as she asked and held on to the wall as she searched my bags. I noticed she took extra sugar and a few oranges. "The rest of you men in line, if you have sugar or fruit, toss them out!" she yelled out to the rest of the kitchen workers in line.

"What's up Ms. Sandoval?" yelled an older Black inmate.

"I got Sacramento Prison board members taking a tour, but you didn't hear me tell you this, got it?"

The Black inmate stepped back in line and said, "Copy that."

She began to pat me down and what happened next caught me by surprise. As she bent down my right leg, gliding her hands, on the way up she grazed my shaft. My immediate reaction was to jerk, but she continued down my other leg. I immediately looked toward the guys to see if anyone caught that, but they were messing around with their bags emptying out oranges and sugar.

"Okay, Rocha, you're good to go," she said, wearing a mischievous smile.

I grabbed my bags and smiled back. "See tomorrow, boss lady," I said, as I walked out.

I was still in shock. I must have had a smile from ear to ear. As I headed toward Spider, I saw him sitting alone and the realization of what was about to go down shook me out of the experience I just went through.

"Sup dog?" I said, as I approached.

Spider got up and fist bumped me. "What up homie, Stranger had to feed the sharks, he'll be back out next unlock."

We sat down, and talked while we waited for Stranger to come out into the yard. I couldn't stop thinking about what had to be done. *This was fucked up.* It's not like we had a year to think about it. We probably had just a few days, if that.

"What do you think about him, Fernando?"

"He seems like a righteous guy," I replied. "He's just like the rest of us, just happened to be at the wrong place at the wrong time. I wish I knew what to do about this. I was thinking we reason with the shot callers, see if there's another solution to this matter."

Spider's face lit up. "You're right, it doesn't hurt to ask." Spider looked like a load had been lifted off his shoulders.

"Hey homies, what's up?" Stranger said, as he walked towards us. "I brought you guys some brownies that my girlfriend sent me. I really don't like them, but I thought you guys might."

He was such a kid, I thought, as I snatched the box from him. "I love brownies," I said to Stranger. *Damn, I was just a kid too.*

Spider wasn't interested in the dessert. He right away went into drilling Stranger with twenty questions: he asked him why he was here, how long they gave him, who he shot, and so on, and so on. He was like a cop interrogating a suspect and I understood why. He was fishing for something that Stranger would say in order to get both of them off the hook. Even though Stranger was young, he wasn't stupid. He had an idea that he was in deep shit. He had been around the block before and he kind of knew how these things went. He was however, a little naïve about exactly how much trouble he was in. Powerful people wanted him dead—it was highly unlikely that he would escape their wrath. None of it was good and solutions were slim.

With great despair, Stranger explained everything in great detail as Spider and I listened. He told us what it was about and who was involved, and just as I had suspected, it was a mistake that the girl had been shot. Apparently, she was mixed up with the wrong crowd—dealing dope and slamming heroin. *Who knew that she would be there that fateful night?* She too, had ended up in the wrong place at the wrong time.

"Look Stranger," Spider said. "We both agree that it's really not your fault. It could have happened to anyone."

"It doesn't make you a bad guy," I chimed in. "It's just that we have to find a way to convince these guys and to see if they could let you make it up or something."

"Don't worry, little homie, everything is going to be fine," Spider said.

Spider was lying about everything. He had been in the system long enough to know how it all worked. He knew it wasn't going to be fine and the shot callers knew that Stranger had to be dealt with. The guys who ran the yard were clear about what was going to happen. The inmates in the yard were all waiting, and Spider more than anyone, knew that there was no turning back. "Yard recall, yard recall!" the yard speaker announced. We all walked back to our cell block. I noticed all the homies on the yard looking. Like buzzards standing around waiting for death.

CHAPTER 17

L ater that night, Stranger didn't come out to yard. He stayed in
to make phone calls. Meanwhile, Spider and I headed out to
talk with the yard's shot caller, Rhino. Spider and I were headed
towards the baseball bleachers. That is where Rhino sat. Rhino was
one of the older inmates and he was one of the top guys who ran
this particular yard. He sat with about a half a dozen other old-timers smoking cigarettes and bullshitting. He was 6 foot, heavy set,
had a large mustache, and tattoo's covering both his arms. A pair
of Ray-Ban sunglasses covered his eyes adding to his sinister look.

The more I thought about it, the more the idea grew on me. Of
course Rhino would understand the situation with Stranger. He had
to be a reasonable man being in the position that he was in, and
I'm sure he had made a few mistakes in his younger years as did
all of us. *Maybe there was some way that Stranger could work this
off?* We walked to about ten feet from the group and waited out of
respect for Rhino to finish his conversation. When he was done, he
acknowledged our presence by looking straight at us. Spider spoke
first. "Rhino, can we have a word with you?"

Without much exertion he excused himself from the older guys
that he was sitting with and walked towards us. Holding his coffee
cup in his left hand, his face was expressionless as he approached
us. With his right hand, he motioned us to walk with him. We only
moved over about ten feet further, but it was a show of respect for
us as we were clearly out of earshot from everybody else. Spider

began his request by letting Rhino know that he had much respect for him. With cleverness, he disguised the compliment. Rhino knew everything that went on within the yard, in other prisons, and out on the street. Spider simply led the conversation by acknowledging that.

"Rhino, it's about my homeboy, Stranger."

"Yes, I know," replied Rhino. His response teetered on being humble rather than arrogant.

"Look, he's a good homie, shit like that could've happen to any of us," Spider pleaded.

Rhino stood with him arms crossed. His chin was up and his head to the side, staring at Spider. "I understand all that. Like most of us, he messed up, but this is above me. It's not coming from this level," Rhino said.

"Is there anything that he could do?" asked Spider. His voice held a pleading undertone to it as he tried to shuffle the fate of Stranger's life and his.

"Is there something that we all can do to make this matter right?" I said, interrupting.

Rhino took his Ray-Bans off and rubbed his eyes. It was a bold move on my part. In Rhino's eyes, I thought I saw a glimpse of admiration. Anyone who would go that distance for his homeboys had to have somewhat of a stand-up character. Either that or he was just crazy.

"Look, you guys don't have to handle this matter. Someone else could handle it," Rhino said, as he turned his attention back to Spider.

"No, no, no. We're going to handle this," Spider quickly retorted.

Rhino shook his head and paused for a moment and then he looked straight into my eyes. "But look, I'll see what I can do."

With that he took a sip of his coffee, put his shades on, turned, and walked away. *If Rhino couldn't do anything for us, what could we do?* We both knew how the system worked. We do it or we'll get done. As we started walking back to our cell block my name was called on the intercom. "Fernando Rocha, report to R & R," (receive and releases).

"Go get your package, dog," said Spider.

We fisted bumped.

"I'll talk with you later, keep your head up, we'll handle this shit," I said.

As I walked into the R & R building, I passed by the cage that I was first held in while they processed us. Two correctional officers stood outside the cage with us inmates collecting our stuff. In the middle of the cage was a three by five foot opening where they would pass the packages to us. From there we would take our package and open it on a separate table and display it to the correctional officers watching us. Everything had to pass their inspection in order for us to take possession of it. I was next in line when the C.O. handing out the packages received a message over his walkie-talkie. "115 incoming, transfer, Ten four," he said, as he depressed the button on the hand-mic attached to his collar. "Take it into the holding cell!" he yelled to us inmates. "Take it to the holding cell!"

Slowly in tow of the other guys, I started to shuffle to the holding tank. "Clear for transfer. Clear for transfer," a voice was booming in the background somewhere. "Face the wall. Face the wall," yelled the C.O., who escorted us into the holding tank. Since I was the last one into the holding cell, I wasn't exactly up against the wall, but facing another inmate's back. This allowed me the opportunity to stand a bit crooked. Then the curious kid in me took over and I adjusted my head to see who was walking by. Then I saw him: one of The Devil's henchmen in person.

With four huge C.O.'s escorting him, he looked tiny. He had shackles. He walked slowly. Then as if he knew someone was staring at him, he looked up as he shuffled by. Immediately our eyes met. I couldn't believe it. That old wrinkly face, his eyes burning with hatred, a swastika tattooed in the lower part of his forehead. I had heard about him from school and the news growing up. Now he walked by just ten feet away from me—Charles Manson, in the flesh.

CHAPTER 18

Charles Manson lives in protective custody within the S.H.U. He had been placed there by the system simply because he wouldn't live a day out in the general prison population. If accessible, everyone would be trying to kill him. Instant fame and celebrity status would come to you. Once he passed we were given our packages. As I walked back toward my cell block, I thought about the situation between Spider and Stranger. The rules were intact and unabated. I knew that nothing was going to change.

It had been two days since we spoke to Rhino. Word had traveled fast. There was talk on the yard, and some of the homies started to wonder if we'd be able to handle it. Immediately, we were being pushed between a rock and a hard place. Then the next morning as I was setting up my work area, Ms. Sandoval approached.

"Rocha, there's a spot available as a grill cook, would you like it?" she asked.

She stood about arms distance, but I could smell her fragrance. "Sure, sounds cool," I said.

She smiled. "Good, I'll put you on the schedule you can start Monday."

As I was tying my apron, she walked away. I couldn't resist looking how her uniform was particularly tighter than most days. She turned around as if she could tell I was looking and caught me staring at her butt. I played it off and immediately looked away. I began washing pans and every chance I got to see her, we exchanged a smile. I felt like I was back in high school; all the feelings, and weird thoughts about hooking up with her crossed my mind.

After work, I purposely made it an issue to be the last one out. She noticed I was in the back of the line and we made eye contact, as if we understood each other's thoughts. I smiled, she smiled. One more inmate in line before me and she didn't even search him, but waved him out. I thought it was meant for both of us, so I followed suit. "Wait a minute Rocha, not you, hands against the wall," she said. The other inmate laughed as he stepped out, clueless of what was going to go down. She stuck her head out to yard, closed the door, and locked it. She faced me, pulled me towards her, and we began kissing. We both were doing a lot of heavy breathing and touching. I rubbed my hands on her back and made my way to her back pockets. *The firmest ass I've ever felt.* She reached down and grabbed a handful of my hard shaft and squeezed it. As I reached in between her legs she grabbed my hand. "No, that's enough, you have to go now." She unlocked the door, stuck her head out to see if the coast was clear, and said. "Okay, you can go!" I got myself together, we kissed once more, and I headed out.

I couldn't believe what just happened. When I got to my cell, Chico was already there. I couldn't shake the smile off my face, and Chico noticed.

"Sup with you?" he asked.

I turned to face him. "Nothing, why you ask?"

"You got this funny smile, what's good?" he asked.

I walked to the cell door, looked out to see if anyone was on the tier, and sat next to Chico. "Check it out Chico, this stays between us, cool?"

He sat up. "Yeah man, of course," he said.

I began to share my involvement with Ms. Sandoval. He stood up to double check the tier. "Who else knows?" he asked.

"Just you, I haven't told Spider yet," I replied.

"Don't tell anyone else," he said. He sat back down. "Look, that's cool and all, but you have to remember, *they* are the enemy." He went on to explain the risks. "You see, a lot of these *vatos* you work with, if they see some funny business between you guys, they're going to hate."

I nodded as this made sense.

"I would suggest you not get involved, but shit, you already swapped spit with her, fuck it, go for broke!" he said, as he gave me a fist bump.

"You're right, Chico, I'm going to keep this low, and besides, with what's happening with Stranger, shit my go south real quick," I said.

Our cell door popped open. "YARD IS OPEN, YARD IS OPEN" came from the intercom.

"I'm staying in tonight, cellie," Chico said.

I put on my jacket and headed out to yard. "Alright, Chico, I'll talk to later."

That night, Spider and I went to the mess hall for movie night. Every now and then they'd bring in a video to watch at the mess hall. We went for the distraction; we also knew that Rhino would be there and we needed an answer. Stranger had become a regular phone monster. He too didn't go out to yard that night. The pressure for us to carry out our mission was mounting. It was crowded by the time we got to the mess hall. We looked around for a good seat. It wasn't like a movie theater where the guy sitting in front of you was a foot lower. Everyone here sat on the same level; on the same chairs that we ate our breakfast, lunch, and dinner. Finding Rhino was more important than prime seats, however.

I was the first to spot him. He was towards the front, near the screen. Once again he was surrounded by the same old-timers that

I saw him out in the yard with. I tapped Spider on the shoulder. From about ten feet away Rhino looked at us and acknowledged our presence. I nodded my head as if to greet him. He knew what we needed to know and he didn't spare us any of the formalities. He simply looked at us and shook his head in a negative manner. Then, it seemed like as if he was doing it in slow motion, he rubbed the palms of his hands together. First right over left and then left over right, as if he was brushing something from his hands.

I couldn't believe it. There was nothing he could or *would* do. Stranger had to be dealt with. Spider didn't even watch the movie. He just walked out of the mess hall. I sat there for a bit staring into the screen not watching the movie, thinking about how soon this was going to play out. I snapped out of it and I caught up with Spider. He was at the bleachers, sitting alone. I approached him.

"You good, dog?" I asked.

He stood up and faced me. "It gets done tomorrow."

I didn't say anything. I just nodded my head. We headed back to the cell block and he explained the hit.

"Once you get him out to yard, as soon as he steps out the cell block, I'll come from behind," Spider said.

"Soon as I get back from work, I'll pry him off that phone and drag him if I have to, out to yard," I said.

***

The next morning at work, I had bubble guts. I must have taken a dump like five times. My nerves where killing me. Then, just as I was cleaning my area to leave, Ms. Sandoval walked up.

"Hey," she said.

"Sup, Ms. Sandoval?" I replied.

She looked around to see if any inmates were looking. "I want you to stay after work and help the back dock guys."

I knew she was bullshitting in case anyone heard, but I knew what she wanted. I smiled, but I had to help Spider. "Ah shit, I have to do something important right after work, Ms. Sandoval," I said.

She didn't like that response, I could tell by her facial expression. She looked around, then walked up on me and leaned into my ear. "I want to feel you deep inside me, and *that* should be more important," she said, as she exhaled a soft moan into my ear.

HARD AS A ROCK. I stood there leaning up against the sink trying to hide the Loch Ness monster. She walked away as other kitchen workers passed by.

It was getting close to end of shift. Part of me wanted to stay back and experience this explosion with Ms. Sandoval, but Spider needed me and I couldn't let him down. I finished up early and paced around the back dock till end of shift. I noticed all the back dock workers were leaving.

"You guys off already?" I asked, as another inmate walked by me.

"Ms. Sandoval has to leave early and sent us home," he replied.

I walked back to my post and noticed most of the kitchen workers lining up to check out. As I made my way to line up, Ms. Sandoval walked up beside me. "Rocha, help me move some boxes please," she asked. I walked behind her toward the walk-in pantry. As she unlocked the door, I looked back to see if anyone could see us. Then she motioned for me to be quiet and walk in. As soon as the door closed behind us she said, "Let's try to make this quick, okay?" Her pants came off and she bent over in front of me. *Make this quick?* I thought, shoot, I just about finished without her. The passion was intense. I felt like I was lifting her up with all my shaft strength. She began to scream and I covered her mouth with my hand—then, the duel explosion. We straightened up and I grabbed some random boxes. She opened the door, checked if the coast was clear, and I walked out first.

It was unlock already and I needed to be one of the first in line. I didn't want her to show me favoritism and have the guys think something was up between us. So, I had to wait. My heart was racing for so many reasons. The thought occurred to me about how I was going to convince Stranger to go to yard. The line was getting closer and Ms. Sandoval shot me a sexy smile. *Three more guys to go.* Then, the craziest and stupidest thing popped into my head: *maybe I could ask Ms. Sandoval to have him called out?* Finally, I was the last to be searched. She waited for them to walk out, then as before, locked the door and we began kissing. I stopped her.

"I loved the way you felt inside me," she said.

I kissed her forehead. "You were amazing," I said.

She pulled away to open the door. "I don't want to do this anymore, okay? Don't expect this again," she said with a smile.

"I agree, this can never happen again," I responded.

We both laughed and as I was making my way out, I asked her, "Ms. Sandoval—"

She interrupted, "Call me Debbie, that's my real name."

I smiled.

"Okay, cool. Debbie, can I ask you for a favor?"

She turned the smile into a frown. "What? Look, I'm not bringing you drugs or any contraband so don't even think to ask!" she remarked.

I had to laugh. "No, actually, it's not like that at all, I have a friend who's looking for a kitchen job, and I was wondering if you had one available?"

Her smile returned. "Oh! Of course I can help with that, tell him to come by tomorrow so I can meet him," she said.

I noticed our cell block door had opened, and I needed to get Stranger out now. "Well, is there a way you can radio the officer in our cell block to have him come right now?" I said.

She looked at me with concern. "He your homeboy from the streets or something?" she said.

I began to walk towards my cell block. "No, just a good guy I'm trying to help, it would mean a lot to me," I said.

She rolled her eyes. "Oh God, okay, what's his name and bed number?" she said.

I gave her his info and headed out toward my cell block.

There was a group of people, "lookie-looks" as we would call them; just a bunch of nosy guys waiting to see the show. The looks I got from them as I made my way into the cell block were like laser beams. People knew Spider was my dog. They knew I too was involved. Finally, the first person I saw sitting in the day room area, fully dressed, is Spider. I approached him.

"Sup dog," I said, as we fist bumped each other.

"That fool is already on the phone, I haven't had a chance to really talk to the *vato*," Spider said.

I looked over towards the phone and Stranger was sitting there talking away with a smile from ear to ear.

"I don't know how you're going to convince him to go to yard dog, I think I might just do a kamikaze right in here," he said.

I took a deep breath. "Look, I found a way to get him out to yard, they should be calling for him any minute, when they do, we'll handle him walking out," I said.

Spider looked at me confused. "What the hell? How?" Spider asked.

"You packing right now?" I asked.

"Hell y—"

Before Spider could answer, the officer in the guard tower

announced, "Prepare for yard release, also, inmate Cortez cell 130, report to kitchen."

"That's how!" I said.

Spider stood up. "Fuck yeah, I'm packing!"

Stranger had a confused look and didn't get off the phone. Finally, Stranger looked toward us. "They want you in the kitchen, think you got a job homie," yelled Spider. Stranger turned to face the phone and hung up. Spider disappeared. I walked up toward Stranger.

"Sup homie?" he asked.

We fist bumped.

"I think you might be working with me," I said.

We began to walk toward the sally port to exit on to yard.

"Fuck yeah, that would be cool, I was just telling my girl that I needed to stay busy, and off this phone," he said.

I laughed. "Yeah man, the stress box can kill you." I froze after what I said. Spider was a few guys back and it was obvious what was about to happen. Everyone in our cell block was watching. As the gate began to close behind us, Stranger noticed all the lookie-looks outside our cell block. He turned to look at me. I lifted my shoulders as if to say I was sorry. Then Spider came from behind him, with his left arm around Stranger's neck, he pulled him back, and with his right hand began to stab Stranger in the chest. Spider then pushed him toward me and I right crossed him till he fell. Spider ran off one way and I the other. Stranger curled up and all the lookie-looks scattered. I walked towards the water fountain, pretending like I was going to quench my thirst. That was as far as I got.

"Get down! Get down!" a gunner yelled, as he cocked his mini 14 rifle. He was aiming at the direction to where Stranger's body was lying. I turned around to see Stranger lying on the ground, a pool of blood underneath him. His right hand was clutching his right side. I could see Spider about ten yards away and still continu-ing to distance himself. *He had done it!*

The next few minutes were in slow motion. All around me in-mates were hitting the dirt. The gunners in the tower aimed their rifles looking and searching for the perpetrator. Confusion perme-ated through the yard as chaos reigned. The Medical Technician Assistants, MTAs, rushed in with a gurney to assist Stranger and get him off to the infirmary. As they carried Stranger off the yard, I actually felt a bit relieved, even though I knew we weren't out the woods yet. *If he survived, would he snitch? Or maybe some other undercover mole on the yard would give us up?* After a few hours of lying on dirt, we were finally searched and interviewed. Then, we were sent back to our cells for a lengthy lockdown.

CHAPTER 19

T hroughout the lockdown, I wanted to share the experience I had with Ms. Sandoval with Chico, but thought better of it. This was something I had to take to the grave. Involving myself with an officer could have gotten her and I in a lot of problems. It could have also got me killed. She was the enemy after all, and that was a major inmate code violation. I was thinking about her and wondering if she was thinking of me. Finally, after eight days of lockdown the yard resumed normal program. We were released at night, so I didn't have to work till the a.m. I headed out to the dayroom and noticed Spider already at a table with a few homies. As I approached, Spider stood up and met me half way. We fist bumped and did not say a word as if we already knew what each other was thinking. "Yard release!" a loud voice announced from the intercom. Spider and I headed out to yard. We walked towards the handball court and sat up on the bleachers. After a moment's pause, I finally spoke up.

"You good, dog?"

"If it wasn't me, it would have been someone else," he said. "Thanks for helping, dog."

"No problem homie," I replied.

He waited for some guys to walk by us before he spoke again.

"What I kept thinking about all through lockdown was, *how did you get him a job so quickly?*" he asked.

I smiled and took a breath. "Check it out dog, I got to share something with you, but I need your word it stays with us," I said.

"Of course dog, shoot it," he said.

I began to run down everything about Ms. Sandoval. His jaw dropped and he kept saying, "GET THE FUCK OUTTA HERE!" As I continued, he looked amazed.

"So, Chico and you are the only ones that know, but Chico doesn't know I've piped her down," I said.

"Don't worry dog, that shit stays between us, but you got to be very careful, you know how these haters are," he said.

I shook my head. "Yup, I know," I said.

From a distance we saw Rhino and his crew walking towards us. "Ah shit, here comes these motherfuckers," said Spider. Rhino and his crew sat with us on the bleachers. We all exchanged fist bumps and handshakes.

"*Quvo* homies, I hope I'm not disturbing you *vatos,*" said Rhino.

"Not at all big dog," Spider responded.

"I was wondering if I could talk to Spider, alone, for a few," Rhino asked me.

"Oh for sure big homie, no worries, you guys handle your business," I said. I got up, handshakes all around. "I'll catch you later Spider, I'm going to library for a bit," I said.

"Cool, talk later, dog," said Spider.

I was glad everything with Stranger worked out the way it did. I knew that with the level of respect Spider and I had now things were going to be different. When I got to the library, I saw Chico helping out some guy with his case, he nodded, and I kept walking towards the education department. School in Corcoran State Prison consisted of three classrooms: G.E.D., E.S.L., and the theology program. As I wandered into the classroom area, I noticed that an older Black man I'd seen before. He looked to be teaching a class of about 15 inmates. I stood outside the window watching him speak about some math problems. He then saw me looking and didn't miss a beat. He continued talking as he walked up toward the window I was looking in through. He opened the classroom door.

"There's still room for one more if you're interested?" he said.

"What is it for?" I asked.

"This is a pre-GED test, to see where you're at before taking the actual test in a few months," he said. He handed me a booklet. "Would you like to try it?"

I felt a sudden urge to. "Yeah, fuck it." I grabbed the booklet, and he handed me a pencil. He continued to hand out the rest of the booklets.

"You'll have till yard recall to finish what you can," he said. "If you finish early, close your booklets and leave your pencils next to them, and you can leave. I will give you your result in a couple days."

Looking down at the answer sheet, I realized that I wasn't prepared for any of this. I did my best however, and before long I was finished. I left my pencil on the desk and stood up to leave.

"Hold up youngster," said FM. I stood outside the class, in the corridor hall, and he approached. "Listen, youngster, we have a few spots available if you're interested in getting your GED," he said.

I paused before I responded. "I'd like to, but I already work in the a.m. kitchen crew." I continued to walk away.

"Well, I'll have the test results here in a couple days if you want to see how you did," he said.

I made my way back to the cell block. I noticed Spider and Rhino were not at the bleachers anymore. I made my way up to my cell when Spider walked up.

"So, what that fool want?" I asked.

"Man, they were all on my nuts, talking about they appreciate how it got handled, and whatever I need just ask," he said.

"You good?" I asked.

"YARD RECALL!" a voice from C.O. in tower announced.

"Shit, back to normal program, homie," he said.

CHAPTER 20

It's was earlier than usual when my cell door cracked open for work call. Chico was still snoring, but I walked up to the cell door and stuck my head out to see what officer was working. "Rocha, Ms. Sandoval needs you ASAP!" yelled the floor officer. I immediately washed up, got dressed, and headed out.

I noticed the early morning cooks were already walking in when I got there. Ms. Sandoval was in her office talking to a Inmate Gang Investigator officer. He walked out heading towards me and we passed each other up. He looked directly at me and nodded his head.

"Sup," he said as he walked by.

I kept moving. "Not a damn thing," I said.

Ms. Sandoval waved me over to her office and I noticed some of the cooks were already aware I was there early, and in her office. *This doesn't look good.* I walked into her office.

"Good morning Ms. Sandoval, was there some reason you called for me two hours early?" I asked. She wasn't her usual self and I didn't see any smile since I got there.

"Sit down, we need to talk," she said rather firmly.

I sat across her desk. "What's up, Debbie?" I asked.

Still no smile. "Cut the shit!" she yelled. "Were you involved? Is that why you had me call for him or was it just a coincidence that he got it, right after I sent for him?" she asked.

I held my poker face. "I don't know what you're talking about, and I wasn't involved," I pleaded.

She stood up and shut her blinds so the inmates couldn't see us. I already knew that was a bad move on her part. I sure as hell didn't want to be in her office another second, plus now, she was starting to put shit together.

"Look Fernando, I was questioned a few minutes ago because I sent for him minutes before the incident," she said, as she sat back at her desk.

"What did you tell the investigator?" I asked.

She looked at me as though that was all she needed to know. The question alone confirmed it.

"I fucking knew it!" she said. "You used me, and now you're trying to lie to me."

I stood up, and before I could walk out of her office I said, "You do what you have to do, Debbie."

I began to set my area up and glanced at the other cooks who were just staring at me. Then Ms. Sandoval walked out of her office. "Cooks, line it up!" she yelled out for them to start their shift. "Rocha, you're on grill number 2!" *I guess things weren't too bad after all.* I started my new job as a grill cook and things seemed to be going smooth so far. I wasn't getting the usual smiles from her, but at least she didn't turn me in.

Later that day, as I was cleaning my area, she walked up.

"How'd you like being a grill cook?" she asked.

I looked up at her. "Finally, there's that smile," I said. I continued wiping the counter.

"I'm still mad at you, I thought you were different, but I guess I was wrong," she said. She leaned in closer. "Don't ever use me like that again, got it?" she whispered.

I stood there, and just from her sweet breath, I was aroused. She walked away. I sure as hell wasn't getting any that day. However, realizing what she had done for me, I began to like her even more.

Later that night, Spider and I were walking along the track. Every group of homies we'd pass would now acknowledge us with more respect. A type of level had been achieved and now guys on the yard knew we were about it. As we passed by the library I noticed FM standing outside with some of the guys I took that pre-GED test with. *He must have our results.*

"Spider, I'll catch up with you dog, I'm going to see something at the library real quick," I said, as I sped off in the opposite direction.

"Alright homie, I'm going to head toward the bleachers, see you later," he said.

FM was with one last guy before I got there. "Hey, youngster?" said FM.

"Sup FM, them our results?" I asked. He handed me a paper. I read that I'd scored a 74 percent over all. "Is 74% good?"

FM had a smile like a proud parent. "Hell yes youngster, you did pretty good for the first attempt," he said.

"What do you mean?" I asked.

"Well, that wasn't the actual GED test, but it's as close to it as it gets," he said.

I was actually proud of myself.

"Youngster, you really should think about getting your shit man," he said.

"I'd like to, but like I said before, I work in the a.m., and I'm not sure if I could just quit that job," I said.

"I tell you what, youngster, you come out to the library after work, and I can tutor you for an hour," he proposed.

I stood there a bit confused. "Why?" I asked.

"Why what?" he asked.

"Why are you helping me? Isn't that like breaking protocol or something with you guys?" I asked.

He looked around the yard and motioned for me to follow him. We stepped away from the library area and leaned up against the concrete wall down a ways.

"Listen here Rocha, you have an opportunity at a second chance. An education will get you farther than any neighborhood gang bullshit you might be into now."

I noticed a few homies walked by and glanced over at us puzzled. One of the homies nodded at me as if to ask if I'm okay. I nodded back, presuming everything was good. They moved on.

"I appreciate your concern FM, I do, but let me think about this," I said, as I started to walk away.

He nodded his head. "I'll be there, every night, youngster, if you change your mind." We walked away in a separate direction.

"YARD RECALL, YARD RECALL!" announced the gun tower intercom.

Later that night in my cell, I began to ask Chico about FM.

"Hey Chico, you think it would look bad if I let FM tutor me for the GED?" I asked.

He stood up from his bed to get something from his locker. "What, you want him to tutor you?" he asked.

I explained the results from my test and how FM offered to tutor me after work. "I want to go to school, but I got this job, Ms. Sandoval, and well, you know," I said.

Chico laughed. "Shit, you want it all, don't you?" He faced me. "Look, one thing is fucking around with a C.O., but now you want to be buddy-buddies with another enemy, that doesn't look good," he said.

I walked up towards the cell door, looked out the tier, and faced Chico. "I'm not no snitch or a *mayatero*!" (into Black people) I yelled.

"I know, I know, take it easy," Chico said. "You can do whatever you want cellie, just understand there are lookie-looks around here, all they do is sit there and talk shit about homies," he said, as he sat on his bed. "You do you Fernando, but just know there are people watching."

I turned to face out the cell door. I thought about what I was going to do.

The next day at work was a close call for Ms. Sandoval and I. We'd been having more intimate conversations and our love making had gone to careless extremes. One day, as I was grabbing some potatoes from the walk-in pantry, she walked in behind me. This wasn't our usual get-down spot, but she insisted. Just as I was about to explode my load in her, there was a banging on the pantry door.

"Oh shit!" I said. I hurried my pants back on and she did the same.

"Stay in here and don't come out until I tell you, okay?" she said.

I hid behind some boxes while she unlocked the door.

"Hey Ms. Sandoval, I didn't know you were there, I wanted to grab a few things," an Inmate cook said.

"I'm in the middle of inventory, can you come back in five minutes?" she asked.

"Okay, sure thing mama," the inmate said.

The door closed. "Step out a minute after I do, okay?" she said to me, as she walked out.

I sat there heavy breathing behind some boxes for a few seconds, then I dashed out. Walking back to my grill, I noticed a few of the cooks smirking. *Shit, they must know.* I played it off and continued with my work. From a distance I could see Ms. Sandoval looking. She was wiping her forehead as if it had sweat, and I read her lips to be saying, "that was close".

After work I decided to take FM up on his offer after all. I showed up to the library and found him sitting in a back table reading some book. He noticed me and waved me over.

"So, you ready to get started, or what?" he asked. I smiled, and nodded my head. So, for the next few days I'd meet up with FM after work, or on the weekends. We'd go over the test questions and ones I had problems with he'd explain. He'd show me different tricks to solve math problems and suggest what books to read to help my writing skills. Every now and then we'd get these mean-mug stares from both his people and mine. Spider was aware of what I was trying to do, and he supported it. In fact, he'd started to ask me question about going to school. The days seemed to move along and there had been no incidents since the Stranger hit—until one particular day.

I was in the yard working out. "YARD RECALL, YARD RECALL" a voice from intercom announced. All the inmates were dumbfounded. We didn't know why we were being locked down. All the inmates from work and school were called back to their cells. Something serious had to have occurred. I remember going into the day room and looking at the TV. For a minute, I thought I was looking up at hell—The City of Angels up in smoke. It looked like the end of the world was happening.

"What's going on?" I asked one of the homies next to the TV.

"Rodney King verdict just came in," he replied.

I looked up again to see a White truck driver being dragged from his rig by a bunch of Black guys.

"City's on fire!" the inmate exclaimed.

He got that right. I couldn't believe what was happening: people looting, cars burning, and chaos everywhere. "Enjoy the few minutes you got in here youngster. This place will start jumping off in a bit," said an older inmate. In the time I had remaining, I continued to stare at the TV. A helicopter caught a lot of the riot on tape: a liquor store was being looted, bottles were being thrown throughout the street, and some Black dude launched a brick at the White truck driver's head.

The people running the prison knew all too well that something like a riot on the outside was nothing more than a sign of the demonic rampage that would make its way through here. There were scenes of Black people beating defenseless Mexican and White people alike. They had to keep us separate with TVs off and phone privileges revoked. Some of the inmates probably already saw the incident on the tube. I really didn't understand why they were mad at us and why we hated them. We all shared the same turmoil: poverty, racism, and we made up for the majority of the colors that lived in here. Even though I could have a fleeting thought that we all were the same, the better part of me reasoned that they were my enemy.

The paranoid C.O.'s finally let us out of lockdown after three days. I couldn't wait to take a real shower. As soon as they cracked my cell I made my way to the shower. Suddenly, this huge Black guy dashed past me trying to get to the shower before me. In doing so, he bumped my arm and I dropped my cosmetics. I don't know if I was angrier because he bumped me or because of his arrogance that he thought that he should be the first to shower.

"Hey, you fucking asshole! What's your problem?" I yelled out.

"Fuck you *ese*!" he replied.

"Oh hell nah!" I yelled out. Then I began swinging at him with a right, left, and uppercut.

There we were—square dancing in our boxer shorts. Once the Black guy slipped on some puddle of water from the shower, I took advantage and stomped his head out. Then I heard the gunner yelling, "Get down! Get down!" As he cocked back a mini 14 rifle. I could feel his sights aimed on me, so I dove onto the floor as far away as I could from the Black guy. From a distance, I could hear C.O.'s running towards us to cuff us. Without looking back and with a touch of arrogance, I placed my hands behind my back and simply let them shackle my wrists. I didn't care. I was proud at what I had accomplished—I had smashed that Black guy. I was sent to the hole. My ribs ached from the pounding. After everything was said and done, I still didn't get a chance to take a hot shower. So, there I was again, taking a bird bath in the cell.

The next morning, I was woken up by noise outside my cell. "Wake up, wake up ladies!" a voice yelled on the outside of my cell. "It's breakfast time." I looked out my small cell window frame and saw a couple of C.O.'s pushing a large container. As it turned out, it was a large refrigerator that held our breakfast trays. *Good*, I thought to myself. *At least I'll get a chance to ask for some clothes.*

"Excuse me C.O., can I get some clothes?" I asked.

"I can't do anything until they take you in for questioning," the C.O. replied.

"Well, when the fuck is that?" I asked.

"I don't know, probably in a couple of hours," he replied.

Later the guard who took his shift came to me with a jumpsuit. I knew I wasn't going to be pulled into a lieutenant hearing only wearing boxer shorts.

I think it was nearly evening before I had my hearing. I was escorted to a small room where I was seated across from a large, balding, fat, White man. He had the most nasally voice I'd ever heard and everything about him was messy. The hair that he had was greasy and he had crumbs in his beard. I couldn't tell because he was sitting down, but I bet half of his shirt-tails were hanging out.

"How do you plead?" he asked.

I didn't give him a direct answer. I wasn't about to say guilty or not guilty. "Look man, we had a misunderstanding. It's no big deal," I said. He looked away as if he was bored or had heard this before. "It just came to blows," I said. "I'm not going to kill him, he's not going to kill me."

"Yeah right. There's plenty of that going on in the streets these days," he replied.

I knew what he was saying. There was tension all over the place. A lot of what was happening out there was quickly spilling into here.

"Look, whatever you have to give me, I'll take it like a man," I replied. I had nothing else to say. I wasn't exactly "not guilty".

"Look, I'm going to suspend a S.H.U. sentence on you because you're being direct with me. Next time though—" He didn't finish his sentence. He just started to scribble on a piece of paper in front of him. "Give this man thirty days in the hole," he said.

Shit, this was fucked. It was going to totally mess up my chances at a G.E.D.

CHAPTER 21

L ucky for me, I only got ten days due to overcrowding. The Black guys I fought paroled from the hole. This allowed me to return back to my cell. I think if I had gotten two more days in the hole I would have definitely lost my cell with Chico. Turns out Chico saved the cell from being housed with someone else. As I walked back into my cell block, I could see the mad-dog stares from the Black guys. I knew the fight caused tension on the yard and I knew I was going to hear it. Spider walked up to me first, greeted me, and helped with my stuff up to my cell.

"Good to have you back, dog," said Spider, as he carried my stuff up the stairs.

"Shit, good to be back," I responded.

"I'll catch up with you at dinner," Spider said, as he set my stuff in front of my cell.

Chico was already in the cell.

"Sup, Chico!" I said rather excited to see him.

He stood up shaking his head, and greeted me with a fist bump. "Damn, cellie, I thought we lost you," he said, as he grabbed my things and set them on my bed.

"I'm glad the cell was still available, I thought for sure I was going to have a new cellmate," I said.

"Shit, it cost me three Folgers jars to keep me from getting a cellmate," he said.

I was taken aback by this. "Really? Ah man, thanks Chico," I said.

"Thanks nothing, motherfucker, you owe me three Folgers jars!" he said, laughing.

I began to wash up for dinner and Chico stood by the cell door looking out toward the dayroom. "You know, we had a sit down with the Blacks because of your little shower incident," he said.

"Really?" I asked.

"Yeah, that Black fool wasn't even affiliated with them, he was some Black fool from Chicago, and ran alone," he said. "That don't mean shit, though, you have to stay on your toes, you got it?"

I nodded. "Yeah, I got it." In that moment the cell doors were cracked open. "Chow call!" the C.O. yelled in the distance. As soon as I got to the chow hall I hooked up with Spider. It was good to get some fresh food.

"Hey dog, glad to have you back," he said, as we shuffled through the line. "How are you?"

"I'm good. That Black fool disrespected me. I had to take care of business."

"That's right. Fuck them *changos*," Spider remarked.

I was evolving, becoming institutionalized by the moment. That evening, I ate rather quickly. I wanted to make sure that I still had a spot with FM.

"Dog, I need to talk to FM," I said, as I stood up with my tray.

Spider still chewing said, "*Orale*. You want me to roll with you, hang out till you *vatos* finish?"

"Hell yeah, that would be dope," I said, as we stood up. "I want to see if FM and I are good," I said, as we walked out the chow hall.

"Good to see you back, youngster," a loud voice said from a few tables down. When I turned to see, it was Rhino and his crew giving me a thumbs up. I nodded, and we headed out to the library.

On our way I began to ask Spider questions.

"So, did the shit almost go off with these *changos*?"

Spider still chewing his food, said, "Nah, these fools didn't want none, they didn't even claim that fool you got down with."

We arrived at the foot of the library as we continued to talk.

"Yeah, so I heard," I said.

Walking in, I saw FM at the usual table.

"Alright dog, he's right there, thanks again, I won't take long," I said, as we fisted bumped.

"Don't trip dog, I'll be over there fucking with Chico," Spider said.

I glanced behind me and saw Chico talking to some guys. I approached FM. He didn't even look up when I approached. "So, you done with your bullshit squabbling or what?" he said, before he looked up at me. I smiled, and nodded my head. I sat down, and he still had our work. We continued the subject where we left off. I didn't mention anything about the fight. I wanted him to bring it up, but he never did. Just as we were about rapping up, they announced yard recall. Spider and Chico were waiting for me outside the library.

"Thanks again FM, I really appreciate it," I said.

"See you tomorrow, youngster," he said as he kept walking, not looking back.

Chico was already walking ahead of Spider and I. He was talking to the yard officer, Smith, who worked the library. He was a big, corn-fed, White guy.

"So, how did it go dog?" Spider asked.

"All good, FM's pretty solid guy," I said.

We got to the cell block entrance. Chico had heard me say this and waited for Officer Smith to walk away before he made a remark. "He's solid alright, but he's also our enemy, don't forget," Chico said. Spider and I looked at each other. We gave off the same "he's right" look.

Once in the cell, Chico and I settled in.

"So, are you going to see if you have a job tomorrow?" he asked.

I was brushing my teeth then spit out and said, "I'm hoping she knows I'm back and cracks my cell for work tomorrow."

Chico, laughing away, said, "Yeah right fool, you don't have it like that sucker!"

He kept laughing. I joined him, but through the laughter, part of me knew different. Lights out.

"Early morning kitchen workers, line it up," the tower officer yelled. Soon after, my cell door cracked open.

"This fool!" Chico said, half asleep.

I jumped out of bed, got ready, and headed out. Just before I closed my cell, Chico rolled over, and saw me leaving.

"See you later, sucker," I said.

The cell door shut. Chico gave me the bird.

I got to the main kitchen and I noticed C.O Smith talking to Ms. Sandoval. I began to start my grill, but another cook remarked. "Sup Rocha, she wanted to see you before you start your grill," the cook said. I looked up and C.O. Smith was leaving her office. Then she saw me and waved me to her. As I headed that way, I noticed other kitchen workers whispering and pointing toward me. I made eye contact with a White cook.

"What's up?" I asked him.

He looked away. "Nothing," he said.

I walked in her office, but remained standing across from her desk.

"Sit down," she said.

I looked around, noticed inmate cooks, but they weren't watching us. I sat across from her desk.

"So, are you okay?" she asked, rather concerned.

I smiled. "I'm fine, it's no big deal."

She smirked. "Really, you a tough guy, a fighter not a lover?" she laughed.

I laughed.

"Listen, I had to replace you so you'll be back to pots and pans for a while," she said, as she stood up. "Now come on, get out of my office, I got work to do," she ordered.

I stood up close enough to smell her body spray. "Damn, I missed your smell," I whispered.

As I walked by her, she graced my shaft. I was caught by surprise and looked to see if any other inmates caught it. Luckily, they were all busy working.

Before she closed her office door, I asked, "Sup with C.O. Smith?"

She gave me a look. "He can try all he wants, but doesn't mean he can get *this*," she said, while pointing at her body.

I walked away laughing.

"Ah, that's right," I said.

Things between us were becoming more than just physical. She started bringing me gifts. Things like certain foods, drinks, and our love making was becoming almost regular. Some of the inmates began to spread rumors. Ms. Sandoval and I were getting comfortable, and getting sloppy. Too many close calls; I had to hear it from an unexpected person, FM.

We were heavy into a certain math question when he brought it up.

"Hey youngster, I need to ask you something," he said.

I looked up at him. "Sure man, what's up?" I said. I set my pencil down and he had my full attention.

"Look, usually I don't give a fuck about what I hear on the yard, but well, I consider you my friend, and you know—"

I interrupted, "What is it FM?"

"You fucking with Ms. Sandoval, youngster?" he said, as he stared dead into my eyes.

I couldn't lie to him for some reason, I respected him I guess. I stood up to see if anyone was close enough to hear. Sat back down next to him, and put him up to speed.

Through it all he just sat there scribbling on a paper listening. I couldn't believe I shared more with him than Chico or Spider. Why I trusted him, I couldn't tell you, I just did. I shut the GED book and stood up. I walked around to see if anyone could hear us and I saw Chico with some homies looking through a book. I turned around to face FM.

"You think I fucked up messing with her?"

FM still sitting, "Yes, yes I do," he said, as he stood up and walked toward me.

We both faced the window to the outside yard, watching inmates go about.

"If it comes down to it, youngster, she'll pick her job over you in a heartbeat," FM said. "I've seen it, time and time again," he went on to say.

"Just the other day, she was talking about living together when I get out!" I said.

FM smiled and shook his head.

"I still got a few years to do, and I'm not going to lie to you, FM, but I'm starting to fall for her," I said.

Now he really started laughing. I realized how pathetic I sounded and I started laughing too. He patted me on the back.

"Ah, youngster, I needed that good laugh, thanks," he said. "I'll see you tomorrow, I got to call my daughter before lock up."

I stood there staring out to the yard, watching FM walk back to his cell block. FM was alright. I felt I could trust in him. I watched him walk by some O.G. Black gangsters and I watched how they went out of their way to greet him. He sure must have been a heavy dude back in his days.

"Rocha!" yelled Officer Smith.

I turned to face him. "Sup, Smith."

He waved me out. "I have to lock up early, tonight," he said, as all the inmates in the library were being kicked out.

I didn't want to go back to my cell just yet and we still had a couple hours till lock up. I saw Spider at the handball court bleachers and headed that way.

"Sup Dog, no FM session tonight?" Spider asked, as I walked up.

I shook some of the homies hands first and then sat up on the bleachers with Spider. I fist bumped Spider. "Sup dog, nah, FM had to make a call," I said.

Just as I sat down we noticed Rhino and some of his crew walking up.

"Hey Fernando, when you get a minute, can I have a word with you?" Rhino asked.

"Yeah, no problem," I said, as I stood up, turning to Spider. "I'll talk to you later, Spider."

I jumped off the bleachers and caught up to Rhino.

"What's up, big homie?" I asked, as I got closer to him.

"Hey youngster, you didn't have to stop your convo with Spider," Rhino said.

"No problem, all good, what's up?" I asked rather impatient.

He smiled, as he must have realized that I was a bit nervous.

"Listen youngster, walk with me. I want you to meet somebody," he said.

We walked to the baseball diamond bleachers where there were three guys sitting. Rhino spoke first and introduced me. "Casper, Jojo, this is Fernando." I nodded my head in a greeting. From one of the guys I got a "*quvo*". Nobody said anything for a few seconds.

To me it seemed like eternity. Then, Rhino finally spoke. "I need to speak to Fernando alone." Getting up from the bleachers, Casper and Jojo walked away. Rhino stayed. Rhino and I sat up in the bleachers and he lit a Camel. He looked like a dragon as the smoke seeped from both of his nostrils as he started to exhale. He kept staring straight like in a daze. He didn't say anything. Taking another hit of his cigarette, he finally spoke.

"Fernando, we understand that you are being tutored."

"That's right," I replied.

"Good. Good. That's really good," he said, as he took another hit of his cigarette. "It's good. You are still young. Get your education." He paused. Then he took another hit of his cigarette and continued on. "That shit you got into with that *chango*, that fucked up our visits. They locked us down for the rest of the day because of it. All the visitors were sent back. A lot of drugs didn't make it in," he said as he gave me a stern look.

"It happened so quickly big homie. You know how it is with these fools. I couldn't let him disrespect me," I said.

At this point I felt nervous. *Did I fuck up? Was this going to get me in some deep shit?* Flicking his cigarette into the air, he immediately pulled another one out of the box. He continued to look right at me.

"What are you going to do with your life when you get out youngster?" he asked.

"I really don't know. I really haven't given it too much thought," I said.

His question really took me by surprise. I really didn't know how to answer and then we just sat there in silence again—in what seemed like eternity.

"I understand that the tutor is a *chango*, FM," Rhino said.

"Yeah, that's right," I said. For a minute I thought I fucked up allowing FM to tutor me.

"Well look youngster, if it's no inconvenience to you, we like for you to keep an eye on him. In fact, don't worry about anyone giving you the stink eye if they see you talking to him at the library or anywhere else. You don't have to hide," he said, as he stood up. Before he walked away, he faced me. "Just know you're doing us a favor. Cool?"

"Sure, no problem, I'll keep an eye on him," I said. "To tell you the truth I don't really understand. I only see him when he tutors me. What is it that I should look for?" I asked.

Rhino ignored the question. "This favor you're doing isn't for me but someone above me. Understand?"

I nodded my head that I did, but actually, I had no clue why they wanted me to watch him close. I headed back to the courts, a little dazed and confused. I didn't understand. *What the hell would they want with FM?* He was this old Black guy who wore wire-rimmed glasses and taught classes. Even though he was large in stature, he was the most unpretentious inmate in the whole prison. He was quiet and always seemed to mind his own business. *Sure he helped me sometimes, but what was I supposed to watch out for?*

"Hey Fernando, quick game homie!" Spider yelled and threw me the ball as I got closer to the empty court. Catching the ball with my left hand, I walked into position. Like a basketball player at the free-throw line, I bounced it a couple of times just to regain my concentration. I glanced back to see where Spider was and which way he was leaning. "Hey Fernando, you all right?"

SMACK!

I must have hit the ball as hard as I ever had. It ricocheted off the wall and went flying right past Spider. *My point.* "I'm good dog," I mumbled under my breath.

CHAPTER 22

O ver the next few days, Ms. Sandoval took her vacation. Work wasn't the same, but I was able to finish earlier than usual, and had time to see FM during his last class. I would wait after and help him stack chairs and clean. During this time we didn't talk about the GED. He actually shared more personal things about himself and his views of the world. I continued asking random questions. Plus, I saw it as an opportunity to honor Rhino's favor. Then after we cleaned he took the time to show me a few math pointers. As he wrote, I was still cleaning the tables and stacking chairs.

At first, FM looked at me puzzled as if he couldn't believe that a Hispanic guy was willing to help him. To me, in my mind, it was the least I could do. FM had done more for me in these last months than any teacher tried to do or attempted in the outside world. Of course there was a difference now—I wanted to learn. I wanted to have the patience to learn. I wanted to put in the time to study. FM taught better than any teacher I had ever had. He broke it down into the easiest terms. He broke it down into practical terms. Math concepts became clearer and stuff like geography and history became interesting to learn. FM had a passion to teach and I'm sure that if he didn't end up here at a young age that would have been his calling on the outside. He also seemed to have a passion to want to teach me. To push me to my educational limits and more importantly he was determined that I pass my G.E.D. on his watch.

So much so that the very next day as I was stacking the chairs, he walked up to me and placed the largest, thickest book I had ever seen into my hands. It was a paperback, but it was still was heavy. "Take this youngster. I want you to have it," he said. The book was fire engine red, and on the front cover in white were the letters G.E.D. At that point, I believe my mouth fell open and I must have looked dumbfounded. It was a gift.

"Go on, take it. Take it to your cell. Study it inside and out. Take the practice quizzes at the end of each chapter and when you finish, take them again. Don't give up until you know everything that is in here like the back of your hand. These are examples of what your high school equivalency test is going to look like. You'll be more than prepared if you put some time in to this. But just don't put *some* time into it, put *a lot* of time." He hesitated for a second and then said, "Put all of your time. It will be worth it."

"Okay," I replied uncomfortably. It was obvious that obtaining this book wasn't easy for FM. He either had to get it delivered by a family member or had to barter with another prison or C.O. to attain it because there was no such amenities in the prison library. I turned the book over. The price tag of the book, right next to the ISBN number, read thirty dollars. In turn, this probably meant that FM was sacrificing something in here like ramen, a candy bar, or cigarettes.

"FM, I can't take this," I stammered.

"Well what the fuck am I going to do with it?" he said in an angry tone.

For him to teach me is one thing but to accept gifts from a Black man was another. I wasn't racist at heart, but I was in a world where I *had* to be to survive. If a little thing like this sounds complicated that is because it *was*.

"Listen to me now, and listen to me good youngster," he said through gritted teeth. "You're young and one day you're going to walk the streets again. Don't let your foolish *Brown Pride* stand in the way of you getting your education. It's all you really got good going on in here." He relaxed his facial muscles and took a step back. "Most of the guys in here when they leave, they always find their way back, and that's because when they get out there they have no foundation to stand on. Their foundation is drugs, stealing, or whatever scandalous mess they can get themselves into. The man who runs this place doesn't want to rehabilitate no matter what color you are. The only way to beat the system is to one day leave the system."

At that point he handed the book to me again.

"Take the book youngster, take it," he said.

I quickly grasped the book from him as he shoved it forward. I felt the exchange was enough of a thank you to him, so I said nothing. I wasn't comfortable accepting the book from FM, but I was also very grateful to have it in my possession to guide me along.

At that moment, an officer Smith walked into the classroom. "FM, time for your board hearing," Smith said. FM didn't even really look at the officer as he walked to his desk slowly and with serious intent. Picking up a pen he walked to where the officer was standing patiently waiting for him.

"I'm refusing again. Where do I sign?" FM asked. The officer marked an "X" on the clipboard and handed it to him. FM scribbled his signature, handed back the clip board and the officer was off.

"FM, why are you refusing your board hearing? Isn't that where they determine if you qualify for parole or not?" I asked.

He looked up at me. "Yes it is, but I gave up a long time ago. These White folks aren't going to parole a Black, cop-killer."

My eyes lit up. I couldn't believe FM was finally sharing his reason for his life sentence. I didn't know what else to ask or say. I stood quiet. Part of me wanted to hear every other detail about his case, but I knew it would be improper and disrespectful to ask him any more questions. Without me saying another word, he was about to elaborate more when a group of older Black gangsters walked by the class and motioned to FM by raising their fists in the air. FM replied to them by giving the same gesture. Right then I knew that FM wasn't just your average tutor; he was someone who still carried a lot of respect from his peers, a "shot-caller" if you will, without being fully active. Later that evening, I found myself walking the perimeter of the yard. Normally I would have been playing handball with Spider, but tonight I declined.

I told him that I must have strained it in the last game. More accurately, it was my brain that was strained. My head was full with so many conflicting thoughts that I just wanted to somehow straighten them out. Plus, it was one of those nights where I really missed home, really hard timing it. I had walked so far from the homies that I was on the opposite side of the yard. As best as I could tell, the Whites were on my right and the Blacks were on my left. I could have confirmed this by looking, but I didn't want to alert anyone by catching their eyes. I should have been high-stepping it across the yard, but I knew it was important to remain inconspicuous until I reached the homies. So, I remained with my head down, and with a slow purposeful gait, I started the opposite way. That was a complete mistake—I should have actually been high-stepping it.

"Hey *ese*," said a low voice. "You out of bounds." I looked up to see the Black guys who greeted FM in class this morning. They were almost surrounding me. *Shit, this wasn't good.*

"*Orale carnal*. Are you alright?" said a voice from behind one of the Black guys. I looked in that direction only to see Rhino along with Casper and two other guys I didn't know standing a few yards away. For a moment everything froze. "*Carnalito*, you good?"

Rhino asked. Casper and the other homies were locking eyes with the Black guys ready for a sudden move to strike.

"I'm good big homie," I replied.

"Let's take a walk. You can talk with your new *friends* later," Rhino said.

Then, just like the Red Sea, the Black guys parted, leaving a large enough gap for me to walk through. Walking up to Rhino, he put his arm around my shoulder. He was basically showing that I had affiliation with them and letting the Black guys know that I shouldn't be fucked with. Leisurely and slowly we headed back towards the bleachers. While Casper and the other two guys walked a few steps backwards as they continued to mad-dog stare the Black guys, Rhino said, "Youngster, you got to be on your toes. Can't be slipping like this." I felt like I was getting a scolding, and I guess I was.

"I got you big homie. My bad. I was just lost in my thoughts and walking," I said.

"It only takes a few seconds for these fools to stab and kill you. Remember that," Rhino said.

With that, he shook my hand and I was headed back to my cell block.

CHAPTER 23

The following Saturday, my parents came to visit. As always, I was grateful to see them. The uplifting feeling I got in knowing they were coming to see me however, was short-lived because the visit felt *too* short. Alleviating your loneliness with a dose of your parents or anyone you loved was never without its own unique hangover or side effect. Once they got here and shortly after the hugs ended, the sadness would start creeping in as the clock would start ticking to the time that they would have to leave.

This would be followed by a huge dose of guilt because I knew that it too put a huge strain on their emotions; not to mention the physical and monetary toll to make the trek. Both of my parents looked tired by the time they arrived and I can only imagine how they felt upon their return home. Many times they would have to find a hotel or motel nearby because given my father's slow driving habits and traffic would make the drive anywhere between four and five hours long. I'll never forget my mom's face the day I walked into the visitor's room. Her smile lit the place up like a Christmas tree as she kissed me from cheek to cheek—tears pouring from her eyes.

I will also never forget that day because just by chance, FM happened to be in the visitation room at the same time. He was sitting opposite to a woman who I guessed to be somewhere in her mid-thirties. With her was a little boy. If I had to guess, I would say he was around four or five. What I didn't have to guess about was that he was bored out of his mind and that the woman and FM were having a heated argument that they were desperately trying to keep private by whispering. Seeing me, he nodded his head in a gesture of friendship. I reciprocated the same gesture as I settled into my parent's visit and tried my best to absorb every cherished moment about it.

My mom usually spent our visits following the same pattern: she talked about our immediate family and filled me in on how everyone was doing. This part of the conversation was combined with her crying and letting me know how much everybody missed me. From there, the conversation would move on from aunts, to uncles, to cousins, and followed by stories and gossip about the neighborhood. It is at this point that my mother became very animated in her story telling, almost as if she were directing her very own soap opera. I liked this part of the visit because I felt it was the only time during the visit she let go of her worries and problems and let everybody else have them instead.

As I listened intently to my mom, out of the corner of my eye I could see the young black woman who sat in front of FM get up in a fit of rage. She slapped the palm of her hand on the metal table several times and then she grabbed the little boy with the other hand to lead him out of the visitation room. I could see FM lifting up his arms in a futile plea of asking her to stay, but she wasn't having any of it.

It was already hard enough if a family member left on a good note, but to leave on a bad one to me would simply be unbearable. The visit was over, and we said our goodbyes. "Take care of yourself son, God protect you," she said. My father didn't talk much, just a pat on my back as they walked away. The next day, I met up with FM after work.

"Your mother loves you very much," FM said, not lifting his head or taking his eyes off the papers he was correcting.

"Yes, I suppose she does," was all I could say.

We had just finished cleaning the class. I was folding the chairs up against the wall, still trying to wrap my head around today's lessons, and now FM had switched gears and had taken them another way. "She really does Youngster. You should appreciate that," he said. I was starting to get a little annoyed at his insistence about wanting to talk about it. I wasn't missing my mom or home on this particular day and I didn't want to start now.

"Who was that woman you were with?" I blurted out in an attempt to change the subject.

"That's my youngest daughter, Melanie. She is the only one who still comes to see me, but that looks as though that might be changing too."

"No disrespect, but why was she so angry?" I asked. As soon as I asked it, I regretted it. FM paid no mind to me asking these types of questions however, and simply answered me right back.

"She gets upset that I have been denying my parole board hearing. She says that if I am going to give up that she might as well give up, too," he said as he stood up to sharpen a pencil. "She reminds me of all the people, my older children included, who have given up on me till this point. She says that if I give up too, then why in the world should she hang on?" he said, blowing on the sharp tip of pencil. "I guess she has a point to all of this."

I nodded my head in agreement.

"But you know how it is in here, youngster. You never really want to hold onto too much hope. Especially when there is not too much to be had," he said.

At this statement I also nodded my head in complete agreement. "Couldn't you just pretend that you were going to them, desperately trying to gain your freedom?" I asked.

"I guess I could," he said, deeply contemplating what I had just said. "It's just that Mel and I have always been very straight forward with each other. I would hate to have to start lying to her now."

For the next couple of minutes we just sat there in silence, both of us chewing on our thoughts. Then I spoke.

"Well, the way I see it, you really only have one clear choice."

"And what would that one clear choice be then, youngster?" he asked.

"You keep going to see the parole board, no matter how much false hope it brings you. Even though it brings you disappointment on one end, on the other end it brings her, your family, and I am guessing that, that is your grandson, some hope." I paused for a brief moment to get my thoughts in order. "No disrespect FM, but, don't let stubbornness and the corrupt evilness of this system break her heart too," I said.

For a minute there I thought I had let my words take a step too far. Then slowly, I saw a thinly veiled smile cross FM's face. "I guess you are right, youngster. I guess you are right."

In that moment, based on my advice, he would make every effort to see his daughter again.

Returning to my cell that evening, Chico had a shit-load of questions to ask me. At first it started off like simple small talk: he started asking me how the tutoring was going, he was asking if I was studying hard for my G.E.D. etc. Immediately, it struck me as funny. *Since when did Chico give a care so much as to what was going on in my life?* The answer was never. This was all about him.

Knowing this early on, I went along with this charade of him caring about me and his curiosity about my education with a nonchalant attitude. For the first five minutes of the conversation I thought his eyeballs were going to bust out of their sockets in frustration as I only supplied him with one word answers to most of his questions while I pretended not to understand others. All that beating around bullshit about *how is school? How is my education going?* lent its way towards what he really wanted to ask: questions about FM.

Did FM say this? Did FM say that? Did FM mention this guy? Did FM mention that guy?

Now my head was swimming and my eyeballs were about to pop with all the questions that Chico was throwing at me. It was almost as if he was bipolar. Some questions were asked in a tone so cool and calm that he almost didn't seem to care if he learned the answer or not. Other questions were approached in a maniacal type of frenzy that life or death depended upon even having a small clue about it.

Finally I broke. Mainly because I was getting annoyed at the stupidity of the conversation, of us not being direct with one another. The other reason was because I realized that maybe I too should be a little scared of the underlying premise of Chico's questions. After all, it was obvious that he was a bit scared or apprehensive about what was going on, and he obviously felt that I could provide the missing puzzle pieces of what was going to happen. "What's up, Chico, spill it!" I said. For the next several hours Chico spilled all the information he knew.

Having full access to the library, Chico could get his hands on lists and transfer logs of several prisons. From what we could best determine was that there was a strong possibility that a powerful and influential Mexican shot-caller was being transferred here. His name was Topper. We also determined that having the same access to the library, FM could have the same information to.

What Chico was hoping I would be able to provide the answers for was if FM voiced any concern about it all. Perhaps at this point in FM's life he didn't pay too much attention to what or who was coming and going through these prison walls, but that was the little tidbit for our sakes that we needed to figure out.

You see, this guy Topper and FM had a feud going as far back, and just as hateful, as the Hatfields and McCoys. As Chico explained to me, no one really could recall the true reason of why it started, but everyone knew of the bloodshed by the soldiers dedicated to each of them along the way and through the years. Chico even went on to describe an old school knife-fight type ritual where they tied one of FM's wrist to Topper's wrist with a bandanna while their free hands wielded a knife chopping at each other's skin and vital organs. Till this day, and because of it, Topper walks with a limp due to a gash of his sciatic nerve and FM dons the scar from a bullet delivered from the gun-tower as he decided not to yield to the threats of getting shot down.

"Oh shit, really?" I said, after hearing all this. "So, what now?"

"I guess we'll find out soon enough, these guys are old battle cats, who knows if they'll still want beef with each other," Chico said.

If Chico's predictions, calculations, readings were right and Topper *was* headed this way, this prison was about to get popping. Someone was going to have to get their hands dirty before it was all over and why Chico thought that it would be his hands was beyond me. Sure, he sometimes shared the library with FM, but I was FM's student and he was my very own personal tutor. It was *I* who was asked by Rhino to keep an eye on him. This all started to come together in the most fucked up way for me. "Lights out," yelled the officer. I thought as I laid awake that evening, knowing that it was I who was going to have to learn of FM"s knowledge, temperament, and readiness of what was about to come.

I got a sneak preview into this world a few days later as I walked into the library and saw FM reading one of the prison transfer logs.

"Everything alright?" I asked in a nonchalant manner.

"Yeah, everything's good," he replied. "Just expecting a few old lifer friends."

He pushed the logs aside and we got to work. Later that day as I was leaving the library, there was a loud voice on the intercom.

CHAPTER 24

"Escort! Escort! Make way for escort!" the speaker from the guard tower bellowed. I had plans to meet Spider at the handball courts, but now I found myself in procession with a lot of other men slowly walking to see the newbies entering the yard. There he was: short, muscular, and walking with a limp. I heard a couple of younger guys saying, "There he is. That's him." You'd think a rock star just entered the yard. Maybe in these circles he was. I just wished that he didn't come to this venue to play.

Later that night in the yard, Spider and I were sitting against the cell block sharing a huge tumbler of coffee when Rhino approached.

"*Quvo* youngster," he politely asked. "How's it going?"

Out of respect, both Spider and I shook Rhino's hand.

"All good Big Dog," Spider said. "Would you like some coffee?"

"No, thank you, but can I have a word with Fernando real quick?"

Rhino's question was rhetorical. He was making his command sound polite. Then again, no one was objecting to it either. It wouldn't have been in our best interest to do so.

"Sure, no problem," I said as I stood up. "What's up Rhino?"

"Let's take a walk. I want you to meet someone," Rhino said, while at the same time turning and walking the other way.

Immediately, I locked eyes with Spider. I wanted to express to him a look of confidence, a look of "hey, I got this". Not that he could have done much if I *didn't* have it. I was about to talk to guys that could turn the whole prison on you with a blink of an eye. Shaking Spider's hand, I said, "I'll be right back, Dog."

Turning and taking a few jogging steps I easily caught up to Rhino. My mind raced and swirled. I knew where I was headed and had a feeling what it was about. My legs weren't shackled, my hands weren't cuffed, yet I had no other choice but to walk side by side with Rhino.

We approached a table of four older homies playing cards. I recognized the game they were playing as the game of Spades.

I also recognized the man I saw earlier in the yard. The man with the limp. The man known as Topper. Topper stood up to greet me as Rhino made the formal introductions.

"Fernando, this is Topper."

I extended my hand, "*Quvo* Topper."

We shook hands and he pulled me to the side. "Hey youngster, good to meet you. I've heard lots of good things about you," he said with the deepest scratchy voice.

I thought to myself, *Is he this polite or is he simply buttering me up?* We walked several more yards in silence then he finally broke it to me. "Youngster, I got a problem that you may be able to help me out with. It concerns FM, your G.E.D. tutor." He looked far into the distance for maybe a few seconds. Instinctively, I knew to keep quiet and even though I wanted to get this conversation over with, I told myself to have patience. I knew it was coming. I just wanted to hear it, walk back to Spider, and figure out what to do. "I need to take him out," he said in a very matter-of-fact tone. "I just can't get anybody close enough to him and I was wondering if you could handle it. I hope you understand."

What I understood was that I wasn't being asked at all. His request was an order; eloquently disguised in politeness. I knew from being here long enough that if a guy like Topper asked you to do something, you did it. If you refused, it could prove to be detrimental. Immediately everything made sense. The extra attention I got from Rhino. The day he came to my rescue when I was surrounded by those Black guys, or how he asked me to keep an eye on FM. *All* this was planned. I was being groomed and I didn't even know it. *Was this why Chico was acting so strange that night, asking me all these question about FM?* I noticed him staring at me, waiting for a response.

"I got you, big homie, no worries," I said. He smiled, threw his arm around me and we headed back to the table. I shook everyone's hand, and then Toppers. "Alright homies, excuse me, I'm heading back to the bleachers," I said as I walked back towards Spider. I knew there wasn't any way I could back down now. I noticed Spider was still sitting alone. He saw me walking up and met me half way. "Yard recall!" was announced as Spider walked up.

"Fuck," I muttered, as we headed back to my cell block. "What did I get myself into?" I said to Spider.

"What happened, homie?" Spider asked.

I briefly shared with him what I was asked to do. We got to the entrance to the cell block. We didn't say anything else—too many guys close enough to hear. Spider just kept shaking his head at the news I dropped on him. Just as I was about to walk upstairs to my cell, "Don't trip, dog, I got your back for whatever," Spider said, as he gave me a fist bump and we parted ways.

I walked into my cell, washed up, and jumped on my bed without acknowledging Chico. As I lay on my bunk, my mind was racing with crazy thoughts. Perhaps this was my destiny; a direct result from helping Spider with Stranger, all put into motion the first day I delivered a package for Gilbert. For the first time I had every intention of doing good, like getting my G.E.D., and now that too was playing against me. *Life was crazy.*

"You alright youngster," Chico said.

"Yeah, I'm alright," I calmly replied.

I tried to look inconspicuous like nothing was bothering me, but inside I was screaming. I felt betrayed. I was angry, terrified, sad, shocked, confused, and conflicted. Chico was working me with all his questions of small talk. "Warm night, right? Did you talk to Rhino? You and Spider play handball?" he said. I knew he was fishing for information. Nothing was said for the next fifteen minutes. My head swirled trying to absorb all the information and get my head wrapped around what I had to do.

Then Chico sat on the edge of his bunk and said, "Did he ask you to do, FM?" I had to do a double take. *How did he know?* Then I quickly remembered. Of course he knew what was going on. I'm sure he's known long before Topper even got to this yard. All those questions he'd been asking, he knew that Topper would ask me to do it; I was the only other homie close enough to FM. I jumped off my bunk, and sat on the toilet facing Chico.

"You knew he'd ask me, didn't you?" I asked. "You could've warned me, and I wouldn't have let him tutor me, but you didn't."

"Listen if I was asked to do it, well, I don't think physically I have it anymore. It's been a long time," he said in a quiet, defeated voice. "I'm sorry, cellie, really I am." He continued to say. I stood up and looked out the cell door window towards the gun tower watching the shift change between officers. "I'm going to help you, no matter what!" Chico went on to say. As I watched the officers exchange radios, I thought about it, and Chico was right. I knew he had been in plenty of chaos while incarcerated. His wisdom would be needed.

"Look youngster, I am going to help you so that we make sure you don't get caught." The last part he said really got my attention, and I was listening. "It will be the day of your GED test. I've already got homies on point and ready to go, but the only distraction that we'll have a problem with is C.O. Smith," he said. It was obvious Chico had planned this out for some time. He leaned in closer. "I know C.O Smith is all into Ms. Sandoval, he talks about her all the time to me at work," he said.

"Oh, really?" I said, turning to face Chico.

"Yeah, man, you know that fool has been trying to get at her for some time now, she's just not giving in."

I looked at Chico puzzled. "So, why are you telling me this about Smith, and Ms. Sandoval?" I asked.

He sat back in his bunk, crossed his legs, and took a drink of his coffee before he responded.

"Smith's going to be at the exit door after you do the hit and we'll need him distracted for you to make your exit clean."

I sat on the toilet facing him. I understood, now, what he was suggesting I'd do. "I'm not sure she'll help Chico, she already knows I had her call Stranger out the building," I said.

"Well, that fool's the only one in your way to make a clean get away," he said.

There had to be another way, someone else to distract him. "Lights outs!" a voice boomed on intercom.

The next morning at work, Ms. Sandoval was back from her vacation. There were other inmates in her office talking to her when I got there. They saw me walking up and immediately walked out. I looked at them like "what the fuck?" They just smirked at me on their way out. There was no hiding our evolvement anymore. It was obvious everyone in the kitchen crew already knew, but still, I acted as if nothing. I'd address her and treat her just the same.

"Good morning, Ms. Sandoval?" she smiled, and walked to her desk.

"Good morning, Rocha," she said, looking around before

opening her desk drawer. "I got you something, but I can't give it to you here," she said showing me a small gift box.

I tried to smile.

"Thank you, you shouldn't have," I said. I was happy to see her, and excited about the gift, but I couldn't hide the worried look I had. She noticed.

"What's wrong?" she asked.

I noticed an inmate waiting at the door for her to unlock the mop room. She motioned for him to wait and I turned to walk to the pots and pans area. "We'll talk later, nice to have you back, missed you," I said walking away.

"Missed you too," she whispered.

Throughout the day, I kept trying to replay the words I would use to ask her for help. It was getting close to end of shift and I noticed Ms. Sandoval was waving me to her. There was an inmate in her office already filling in for her clerk. I walked into her office.

"Sup, Ms. Sandoval, you called for me?" I said.

She handed me a medical slip. "They need you to report to medical, ASAP," she said, not evening looking at me.

I grabbed the note and headed back to finish cleaning my area. I opened the note which was stapled and it wasn't a medical note at all. The note read: "I unlocked the walk-in pantry, meet me there in 10, pants off mister! (Wink-smile face)" I didn't even finish cleaning my area. I snuck away so inmates couldn't see me and hid inside the pantry. My heart was racing like always in these moments with her, but this time felt different. I sat behind some boxes and a few minutes later, I heard her opening the door.

"Come out, come out, wherever you are," she said. I stood up and saw that she was holding the gift box. "There you are!" she said. She walked up, dropped the gift bag, and we were all over each other. As we kissed she tried to tell me something. "Umm..

ahh, we have less than…an hour…or so…today," she tried to tell me, as I was kissing and undressing her. It must of been the tension I had or the lack of not being with her for a while, but we exploded together. As we dressed, she handed me the gift box.

"Here, open it," she said.

I grabbed it and unwrapped a box of macadamia nuts. "Hmmm, thanks baby," I said.

"I wish you could've gone with me to Hawaii, you would love it there," she said.

We sat there for what seemed like 10 minutes talking. I wanted to ask her about the whole distracting Smith thing, but I still wasn't confident enough to ask. Her radio went off and it spooked us.

"Okay, baby, let's go before next shift comes," she said.

There, as we headed out the pantry, I asked, "Debbie, I need to ask you for a favor."

She locked the pantry door and we walked out towards the exit.

"What's up, babe?"

I stopped before she let me out to yard.

"I don't want to lie to you, or think I'm using you, but I'm in some deep shit," I said.

"What, what is it?" she asked concerned.

So, I laid it on her. I told her about everything, from Topper, to FM, and the GED test. She just leaned up against the wall, arms crossed with the most puzzled look on her face.

"I didn't want to ask you for this, but Smith is my only hurdle to safety, and he'll be at the door way if not distracted."

She lost it.

"WHAT THE HELL DO YOU THINK?" she yelled.

I grabbed my bags and prepare to head out as she unlocked the door.

"HOW FUCKING DARE YOU, and what, you thought I would do this for you, again?" she continued. She unlocked the door and pointed for me to leave. "GET THE FUCK OUTTA MY SIGHT!"

I nodded my head.

"You do what you have to with the info I gave you, but I trust you, Debbie, that you'll keep this between us."

She said nothing and I walked out. As I headed to my cell-block, I knew I'd fucked up. *Why did I let Chico convince me to ask her, shit, wasn't he the one telling me "she" was the enemy, and all that bull shit?* I was in real deep shit now. Once in my cell, I didn't even mention any of this to Chico. I wasn't going to even mention it to Spider. All I kept thinking was that at any moment they would come for me—her and a few investigators.

Later that night at yard I met up with Spider. He was carrying a small laundry bag. "Sup dog, here, take this back to your cell before they lock the cells for yard." Spider said. I didn't even ask what it was, but I had a strange idea what it could be. As I got back to my cell, I noticed Chico still sitting there reading. I opened it and I tossed it to Chico. "Here, put this away for me cellie," I said just as the officer was walking up the stairs to lock the cells for yard release. Chico grabbed it and stuck it under his mattress. Spider and I went back out to yard. We took some laps till it was time to lock it up.

"Okay, all you have to do is sharpen it, and it's ready to go," Spider said. Revealing what that package was. I didn't say much, just nodded my head. He was running it all down, on how it feels to stab a man. He somehow knew this was my first attempt with a shank. I had used a battery pack before, but never a shank. This was going to be my first of many.

"Once you insert it inside him, twist it some, and strike him again till it's done," he went on to say. Still I wasn't responding.

My mind was all over the place, and he noticed my silence. "I know you have a lot going on right now, homie, but don't worry, it's going to be over before you know it," he said. I finally spoke.

"I didn't go to my tutor session with FM today," I said.

"Why?" Spider asked.

"I was with Ms. Sandoval, and well, you know."

Spider smiled.

"Fuck yeah, she's back, I saw her at chow, man that tan on her makes her look like a Tropicana model."

I smiled, for the first time. As we made our second lap I noticed FM sitting outside the library at the nearest table.

"Spider, give me a minute, let me go talk to FM, real quick," I said.

"Cool dog, I'm going to the handball area bleachers, see you later."

I noticed FM was talking to another older Black man when I approached. "FM, can I talk to you for min?" The old man sitting with him said something to FM, shook his hand and was off.

"Come, sit down with me, if you're not scared to sit with a Black man," he said, rather joking.

I sat across the table. "Sorry for not making our meeting today, I had extra duty at work," I said.

FM smiled, and took a drink of his tumbler. "I bet you had some 'extra' duty," he said.

We both smiled. I noticed his facial expression changed within a second. He was staring directly behind me. I turned curiously and noticed Topper sitting across the yard at a table with some homies. He was staring toward our direction, nodding his head, grinning.

"Sup, FM, you know that guy?" I asked acting curious.

FM took another sip of his tumbler. "Nope, never saw him before in my life," he responded.

Lying through his teeth was something I picked up on. He stood
up. "I got to go call my daughter youngster, make sure you make
it to our meeting tomorrow, big test is just around the corner," he
said and walked away. I turned back to face Topper. He was still
looking in our direction, more so at me now, and nodded his head.
As if to say "good, keep on him". "YARD RECALL!" came from
the loud speaker.

So, later that night Chico and I unwrapped what Spider had
gave me. It was one of those pieces of steel cut from an oven tray
and I didn't exactly have access to a measuring tape, but I esti-
mated it to be between 6½ to 7 inches long. Chico walked over to
the cell door window, explaining where and how much to sharpen
the piece of metal. "Okay youngster, I'll be the lookout," he said.
"Remember, rub it a thousand times on one side and then flip it,"
Chico instructed me.

Behind the toilet was a plate of bumpy granite. Not the most
suitable stone for shaping and sharpening a knife, but the only one
there. Sitting behind the toilet wasn't much fun either. Actually,
in truth I mostly kneeled. It was an archaic method that proved to
be lengthy and tedious. I sat and counted, *one, two, three,* all the
way up to a thousand and then I flipped the rod and started scrap-
ing again. More than once, Chico alerted me to a guard's presence
and I had to stop. Hopping up into my bunk, I hid the shank under
my pillow and pretended to sleep as the guard passed by. Those
untimely visits proved to be a nuisance.

It felt like they counted us almost every hour on the hour. It took
me till 2:30 a.m. to finish the job, but I still had to make the handle.
"Wrap it up tight," Chico muttered. "You've got to get it as tight
as possible, youngster. You don't want it to slip." I produced two
pencils that I got in school. They were held together by tape that I
smuggled from school. I wrapped the tape several times around the

pencils to smuggle it back from school. Basically, I had a couple of mini tape roles at my disposal. The tape was to hold the shoe string securely to the shank. To then thicken up the handle, I rolled several strips of material from a torn t-shirt that was held together by another application of tape. Finally, the shank was ready.

"Come stand as a look out, I want to see it," Chico said. As I stood staring at the officer in the gun tower dozing off in his chair, I could hear Chico. "Ah man, that's nice. Good job, cellie," he said. He put it inside a cereal box and then sealed it back somehow with tape. He put it in the footlocker we store food in and jumped into his bed. "I'll keep it there till the day of your test, get some rest, you'll be waking up in a few hours for work," he said and rolled over to sleep.

I wasn't sleepy, but I sure felt tired. I jumped on my bed and just lay there with my eyes closed, but still awake. What seemed like minutes later I felt myself drift into sleep, but not for long as my cell door popped open. "Kitchen workers, line it up for work!" the floor officer yelled out. As I brushed my teeth, I envied Chico, I could hear him snoring.

I headed out toward the kitchen. All I kept thinking about was what Ms. Sandoval was going say or do. Part of me felt that if she really wanted to fuck me over she'd have done it already. So, part of me felt safe for the most part, *or was I?* As I walked into the kitchen and glanced towards her office, I could see she was talking to another female officer. They both glanced at me and then back to their conversation. I paid no mind and just started my work day. Throughout the day she didn't even acknowledge me or make an effort to look my way. I figured that was it: just the fact that I asked for her help in this broke our relationship off.

Finally, my shift was over. I lined up with the rest of the guys who were heading out. She was searching everyone's bags and dismissing them after a pat down. One cook said a wise crack about me being in line. Other cooks laughed, but I kept my poker face ignoring all the stupid comments these guys were dishing. Not seeing Ms. Sandoval and I talking raised concern among the cooks. They obviously knew we fell out. Finally, it was my turn to get searched. She threw away my bags and when she patted me down it wasn't sensual as usual. Still, not a word was spoken between us. We did make eye contact and I noticed her eyes watery as I exited the kitchen.

I went directly to meet up with FM. Spider was waiting for me after work. He walked me to the library. By now Spider had known everything about Ms. Sandoval and I. We had a brief conversation about her on our way to the library.

"Man, fuck it dog," he said. "I'll have one of the homies cause a scene in front of the library or something," he said.

"I don't know, dog, that doesn't seem like a good idea," I said. "We need that fool away from the library door as far away as possible," I continued to say.

We got to the library entrance.

"Fuck, Spider, I'm not too sure about it, but I can't stop now, it has to get done," I said.

"Well, I'll be waiting for you as I feed the sharks, don't worry homie," he said, turned on his heels, and was off.

I entered the library. FM was drinking water from the fountain when I walked in. "Hey, look who made it today!" he said, wiping his mouth. I smiled and helped him stack some chairs. "Never mind them chairs, save me the trouble of bringing them down for the test tomorrow," he said. I sat down at a desk and he stood at the chalk board. I opened up a workbook and grabbed a pencil from his desk. I noticed the transfer log on his desk with Topper's name and cell number circled. FM walked up behind me and dropped a large folder on top of the transfer log.

"What you stealing from my desk, youngster?" FM said in a joking manner.

"Chill out pops, just borrowing a pencil," I said and sat back down.

He knew I saw the log. In fact, something about the way he spoke to me that day made me feel as though he knew. "Today is our last meeting here together till the test tomorrow," he said. I sat there thinking about what his words truly meant.

"So, how do you feel about tomorrow's…test," he said rather weird.

I looked up at him sideways, trying to read him, and I responded. "It's the first time for me, so I hope I don't fuck up," I said.

FM smiled and blinked his eye. "You'll be alright, youngster, you'll be alright," he said and continued with today's final lesson.

That night Chico and I went over every detail of the hit. We still didn't have the distraction for C.O. Smith, but we figured we'd try to risk it. I slept uneasy; unsure about what I was about to do. Plus, I was taking the G.E.D. exam on the same day. I figured, shit, it really didn't matter anymore if I passed or not. I sure as hell didn't have that on the top of my list anymore. All I wanted was for this to be over and done with. "Lights out!" the floor officer yelled.

Ms. Sandoval knew today was the day of both the hit and the GED test. Part of me wondered why she didn't snitch me out yet or if she was going to wait and catch me in the act. I needed to see her before I went to take the test. As Chico and I were getting dressed for breakfast, he pulled out the foot locker.

"Go keep point cellie," I said as I stood at the door looking out for the officer, while Chico retrieved the shank.

"Here, might as well carry it on you, you're going straight to the library right after breakfast anyway," Chico said.

I grabbed what looked like a make shift dagger and stashed in along my inside jacket. "Chow release!" yelled out the C.O.'s as our doors popped open. As soon as I stepped out to wait on Chico, I saw some of the homies looking at me, all nodding their head in a form of respect. They knew what I was about to attempt, and if successful, it would give me a major rise in status, if not, for sure a death sentence.

We met up with Spider and we walked together to chow.

"So, how you feel, big dog?" asked Spider.

We walked on to the yard.

"I'm a little nervous, I'm not going to lie," I said.

"It's normal, cellie, you'll be okay, don't worry." Chico said as he walked further on with some older homies.

Spider and I were dragging our feet. I wasn't hungry, not one bit, in fact I felt like I needed to use the restroom. These bubble guts were acting up. As we got a few feet to the kitchen entrance, I saw Ms. Sandoval standing outside talking to the same female officer from before. We made eye contact, she motioned me over to her, but I kept walking into the chow hall.

"I think she was motioning to you, dog," Spider said.

"Ignore her, homie, I am," I said.

I wasn't too sure what she wanted, but I had a shank on me and the last thing I need is for her to somehow feel it on me. As we got our trays and sat at our table, she called for me on the intercom to report to work ASAP. "This bitch," I said. Everyone in the chow hall looked at me. That wasn't cool of her. These fools could be thinking anything right about now. I had to make it to take my test, no matter what.

"Just go see what the bitch wants, homie," said Spider. I tried to drink coffee because I didn't have an appetite. Then I caught her looking at me through the window of her office. I could read what she saying, "Come here please!" I nodded to her, "Yes".

"Fuck it dog, I'm going to see what she wants, then heading straight to testing," I said.

"Cool, dog, stay focused remember," he shook my hand, first time ever since I met him, we usually fist bumped.

Then before I could go, Spider said one last thing. "Don't worry, Fernando, I'll be there waiting for you, I got your back, dog," I nodded my head, excused myself, and stepped out. I exited the same way I came in and walked toward her office via the outside door from yard. I knocked and she opened, looked around, and let me in. She had closed her blinds and there wasn't any other inmates close by. I stood there, clueless as to what she wanted. She locked the door and looked out through the blinds before she spoke.

"Are you still going through with it?" she asked.

I rolled my eyes and figured she was going to try and stop me. "Yes, I have to, I have no other choice," I said.

She shook her head and she began to cry. "What the fuck, Debbie, why are you crying?" I said rather confused.

She grabbed some tissue from her desk, looked out the blinds again, and dropped it on me. "I'm pregnant," she said.

There was a few seconds of silence; I couldn't comprehend what she was telling me for some reason. I didn't even consider thinking it to be mine.

"What...," was all I could say.

She nodded her head. "Yeah, I wanted to tell you when I got back from my vacation, but you dropped all that bullshit on me about FM and I just got scared."

I started to feel nauseous. I sat down and grabbed my head.

"Look, it's definitely yours, no doubt about it, just in case you think otherwise," she said.

I looked up at her. "I believe you, it's just, I mean, I don't know what to say or how to feel about this right now," I said.

She sat next to me. "Look, I know I can't convince you to stop what you're about to do, but just know what ever you decide, I'm keeping the baby," she said.

"All GED testing inmates report to the library!" a voice was heard on the loud speaker. I stood up. "I got to go," I said. She stood up to unlock the door, but reached out and hugged me first. I tried to push back, but it was too late. She felt the metal rod along my side jacket. She looked me dead in my eyes before I stepped out. "I love you, Fernando." I felt immediate joy with mixed feelings of anguish and anger combined. I kissed her forehead and was off.

As I walked toward the library, I could see no homies playing handball. Everyone was just leaning up against the wall. *Damn*, I thought, *how obvious the fuckers look*. To my far right, I saw Spider and other homies at a table already waiting. Then just as I got to the entrance of the library, I saw Topper. He was walking laps with his crew when they passed by. "Good luck on your test, youngster," Topper yelled. I nodded and headed inside. I noticed a few guys already sitting with their bubble sheets. I sat down in the back row. FM was talking to the free staff worker and was handed the worksheet.

He walked down the row of seats passing them out. "Don't bother looking at the gentleman's paper next to you because you all have different tests," he bellowed as he walked down the aisle handing out more tests. "When you finish your test, you drop your pencil in the bucket outside with officer Smith and leave your test on your desk for me to pick it up," he said, walking back to his desk. FM picked up a timer. "Okay begin," he announced as he hit the timer.

As I began to fill in the bubbles, I drifted in thought about what I just heard from Ms. Sandoval. I couldn't believe what was happening; the news of me being a father plus the stress I had upon me to kill FM. It was just too much to deal with. It had been two days since I created the shank and now I was expected to use it. *I wasn't' ready.* I just wanted to finish my exam and run out of there, but I couldn't. I had no choice. Before I knew it, the time was close to being up. I had finished the test a while ago and I was just biding my time waiting for the others to get up and leave. I was pretending to think as I watched FM stand up and fold a letter that he had been writing. He looked me straight in the eye as he did so. He never lost eye contact with me as he placed it inside a *prison-mail* envelope. Envelopes used to write inmates in other prisons or within your own—an old system of sending a text if you will.

"Okay youngster, time is up," he said. I looked around and it was only him and I in the room. Quietly, he walked from desk to desk picking up everybody's answer sheet. I got up to leave. I had intentionally left my jacket behind with the shank in it. As I was about to exit the door he called me. "Hey youngster," he said, as he slowly and deliberately walked up to me and extended a hand. "Good luck. I hope you pass your test. Take care youngster," he said. Till this day those words resonate with me. Filled with sincerity, I knew that he wished me well no matter what choices I would make in the years to come—or the next few seconds.

"Hey FM, I forgot my jacket," I said as I returned to the classroom. He didn't even look at me. He just stepped aside to let me retrieve it. Then I couldn't believe what he said next. "Lock the door when you head out, I'll be out in the hall waiting so you can handle your business," he said. The last part was practically a whisper, but I heard it and understood. I ran into the room to get my jacket. I put it on and buttoned it. I couldn't afford to get any blood on my clothes underneath. When I reached the corridor FM was only a few steps down the hallway. His back was turned to me. He did not look back as he was leaning on the wall looking over some paper.

I reached inside the jacket and gripped the shank. Within seconds I was upon him. Unable to stop myself I wrapped my left arm around his head and with my right I stabbed him repeatedly in the neck. Blood splattered everywhere. He started to fall. He was holding on to me as I stabbed him in the ribs and lower abdomen. Looking back, he never struggled against my efforts.

As his weight slumped on me, I bent my knees and slowly, gently, assisted him to the floor. For a second our eyes met and I saw in his face an expression of deep sorrow and infinite regret. Not only for him, but for the both of us. Taking off the blood stained jacket, I threw it over him.

"Sorry FM," I said as my eyes started to well up with tears. "I'm so sorry."

With the last of his strength he pushed me and said, "Go youngster, go, get the fuck on."

Leaving him, I made a fast pace out and down the school corridor. Just a few feet to the exit and I was out. Before I knew it I had made it to the outside bathroom area. I glanced back to see where C.O. Smith was and to my surprise, I saw him and Ms. Sandoval talking a few yards out from the library. She made eye contact with me, smiled at me, and continued her convo with C.O. Smith. *Damn, she came through after all.*

"Give me the shank, dog!" Spider yelled as he sat on the toilet. I gave Spider the shank and he flushed it. Our eyes met and he saw my hurt and understood it, but there was no time to express any of it—I had to keep on going. I took the top layer of clothes off and put them in a trash can near the toilet area. I looked up at the guard tower. As soon as he turned his back I made a dash for the track. I was wearing shorts and pretended I was jogging. Some of Chico's homies ran up by me and jogged alongside me till I was out of range. Just as we got to the end of the track, the alarm went off at the library. "YARD DOWN, DOWN ON THE YARD!" yelled the gun tower. We all dove to the ground. I watched as the officer ran toward the library.

I could see Ms. Sandoval, and Smith were the first ones there. Minutes later, the medics rushed in. As we lay there, I noticed them carrying FM's body out, rushing back to the infirmary. We laid there for about 3 hours or so. You could hear the ambulance driving up to pick FM up. Then, officers from other yards arrived. We were stripped down, searched, and with hands behind our back escorted to our cells.

CHAPTER 25

M y heart was still racing; it was almost as if it was going to beat out of my chest. The first thing I did when I returned to my cell was vomit. I couldn't help it. My chest heaved and my stomach convulsed as I regurgitated every nutrient that existed in my body. Finishing and exhausted from everything that had just happened I sat on the floor next to the bowl, as sweat poured down my face. It was then that I caught a faint reflection of myself in the stainless steel of the toilet and I thought to myself, *What a dirt bag, Fernando*.

The day of the stabbing ended up being a busy day for the prison. The C.O.s were busy playing detective trying to figure out who the perpetrator was. The lieutenant was busy rounding up a satisfactory shot caller from the Mexicans, Whites, and Blacks. The idea was to see if they could find out more info. More importantly, the upper ranks wanted to have reassurance that no retaliation would take place. This basically was a "fuck-off" meeting they would play out for show. It was a formality for the warden to look good in Sacramento. As to what would happen in the future and their ability to keep control, it meant nothing. They knew that. We knew that. So, what followed was a pretty extensive lockdown. They just wanted everybody to cool down and they thought six months would do the trick.

So there I was, stuck with Chico for a half a year. Things were different with him this time around, however. He was a little bit more respectful towards me. Perhaps he was just giving me props for what I had done. Or perhaps now, he was well aware of what I was capable of doing.

As for myself, where do I begin? Some days I didn't know which way was up and which way was down. I hated myself for what I had done, but I couldn't reverse time and I couldn't take it back. I thought about Ms. Sandoval and being a father. I wanted to talk with her, but I knew it was close to impossible. I didn't tell Chico anything about her and felt it best not to tell anyone else. I really missed her and I wanted to see her again.

After a few days of lock-down, they allowed the Whites and others out for the normal program. Blacks and Mexicans were to remain locked down till further notice. That night Chico and I were playing a game of chess when a note slid under our cell door. I jumped up to see who'd slid it through and I saw this big, White biker fool walking away. "It's a *Wila*," said Chico. It had my name on it.

I unfolded it and in very same fine print I read: "Fern, great job, carnalito." It was from Topper. Chico read it and flushed it right away.

"Well cellie, I guess you scored big time with Topper," Chico said.

I sat back to finish playing chess.

"Honestly Chico, I feel like shit for doing FM like that," I said. He made a move.

"Well, look at it this way, better FM than you, *que no*?" he said.

I moved my queen backed by my rook, right in front of his king.

"Check mate," I said.

Then as I was putting the chess pieces away, I could hear a nurse walking through the tiers handing out meds to Hispanic and Black inmates on lock-down. Her voice got closer towards our cell and then I heard someone else's voice with her. It was Ms. Sandoval, she was escorting the nurse. I jumped up and took a peek out the side of the cell door. It *was* her; she was just a few cells down. My heart raced. I was actually going to see her. "Finally, I was wondering when they were going to bring me my pills," Chico said. As the nurse approached, Chico stood at the door while Ms. Sandoval unlocked the small window used to cuff or feed us through. I stood behind Chico, in eye level to Ms. Sandoval. As Chico got his pill and bent down to drink water from our sink, our eyes met. She smiled immediately and I couldn't hold it in either. I had a smile from ear to ear, and she noticed.

Just as Ms. Sandoval was about to lock the small door, as soon as the nurse looked away, Ms. Sandoval dropped a small note into our cell. Chico kicked it over to me and I put it under my mattress until they walked away. "Ah shit, cellie!" Chico said. I jumped on my bunk and pulled the note out.

It read: "After you left the kitchen that day, I don't know why, but I couldn't believe I wanted to help you with Smith. I had to go out to dinner with him, thanks, (sad face) but I let him know I just wanted to be friends. I'm 6 weeks now and pretty soon I'll have to take a maternity leave. I'm so glad you didn't get caught, and don't worry, the investigation stopped, and I hear your guys will be off lock-down soon. Write me back, and I'll pick it up when I escort the nurse again. Miss you, love you, soon to be my baby daddy. (Wink face)"

I jumped off the bunk, flushed the letter, and stood staring out the cell door window.

"So, everything good?" Chico asked.

"Yea, we're good, and she said we might get off lock-down soon."

Chico lay back on his bed and crossed his arms behind his head.

"Fuck yeah," he said dozing off.

I continued to stare out the window. Some of the homies where doing the same and when I made eye contact with them, they all nodded their head to me. A form of respect I didn't have before.

For about the next week or so we communicated through these notes. She wrote about how she measured her stomach and can actually see herself growing. We never brought up the incident with FM anymore. Then one day, she didn't show. I figured she'd taken a day off or something, but the days after, still nothing. Chico noticed I started dragging my feet. "Maybe they transferred her to another position, they do that, you know," Chico said sarcastic. I just gave him a mean-mug look. I wasn't trying to hear that. Truth is, I was concerned about her pregnancy. The days passed, and then months. I soon started to think it best not to worry about her too much. In fact, I stopped thinking about her. I was letting the time do me, instead of me doing the time. So, the days went on.

It was customary for the C.O.s to punish us by holding up our mail. Plus, I believe the lazy C.O.s didn't want to be walking up and down these tiers every day delivering it. So, on this particular day, I got three at once. It was the middle of July, but getting all that mail at once, it surely felt like Christmas. I tossed my *Low Rider* magazine to Chico. Chico rarely got mail unless it was legal stuff, so when he caught it he bounced on his bed like a little kid and started to flip through the pages.

The magazine itself looked like it had been thumbed through several times over, so another time surely would not hurt it. I would get to it later. What I was most interested in was the large manila envelope. Tearing it open, I looked at its contents and could not believe my eyes. A smile gleamed across my face.

"Chico," I called his name lightly just to get his attention.

"What is it cellie? You want your magazine back?"

I heard him close it and then I looked down to see him handing it to me.

"No, you keep it for awhile. I'll get to it later when I can."

I paused for a moment; still trying to take it all in. "Chico," I said again, as I passed him the certificate that announced in bold letters that I had passed my G.E.D. In some ways I had forgotten about it, I was in shock.

The next letter was a prison envelope. I wondered what bullshit is this. After all, I was still in the glow of getting my G.E.D. Unbeknownst to me, I was about to find out that the G.E.D. certificate would pale compared to what I was about to receive and read next. Opening it up I could see that it was FM's handwriting and the first page simply read:

Come now, let us settle the matter, says the Lord. Though your sins are like scarlet, they shall be white as snow; though they are red as crimson, they shall be like wool.
–Isaiah 1:18

Call on to me, and I will answer you & show you great and mighty things which you do not know.
–Jeremiah 33:3

I forgive you,

–FM

After reading the second scripture, all the air left the room. I couldn't breathe. I froze and couldn't flip to the next page. I thought about the last time I heard that scripture and the White guy that prayed for me. What I felt was that my conscience weighed heavy, riddled with guilt.

"What's wrong cellie?" Chico asked.

"Nothing," I replied, as I stuffed the letter between two pages of a book that I had been reading.

I lay there thinking about my life up to that moment. Then to our surprise, the announcement, "YARD IS OPEN FOR ALL

INMATES, YARD IS OPEN!" It was music to our ears from the control tower. Whistles and cheers from my people, and hollering from joy, the Black brothers.

"Dog!" yelled Spider, looking really pale. We fist bumped. "Sup, Spider."

We stepped away from the crowd that was forming around us to talk.

"How are you, homie?" he asked.

I noticed everyone was looking at me. Especially the Blacks.

"I'm not going to lie dog, still a bit edgy." I said. "YARD RELEASE," yelled the control tower as we're released to yard. I noticed our homies hadn't stepped out yet, they waited till Spider and I got there. I looked over at Spider, he lifted his shoulders, and we head out. The level of respect I felt at that moment didn't compare to the depth of my guilt. However, I had leveled up. A mission, fully accomplished, began my new way of life. Spider noticed all the homies first. "Damn, dog, look at all the homie at the handball bleachers," he said. As we walked in that direction, I noticed the groups. As we got closer, all the homies began staring at me. Some older homies walked up who I've never met and shook my hand.

"*Mi respeto carnalito*," (My Respects little brother) said the older homie. Then, Topper, Rhino, and their crew walked up. They all shook our hands and Topper put his arm around me. We walked a few feet away from the rest.

"I'm fucking proud of you little homie," he said, shaking my hand again.

I just nodded and didn't say a word. Inside I was burning mad. I wanted to physically hurt Topper, but I didn't understand why.

"I want to show you my appreciation little homie, I know you're still a youngster, but you have a lot of heart, I like that," he said.

I stood there for about 20 minutes, just listening to what responsibility he was giving me. As he talked, I wondered, *What the hell did I get myself into?* I looked back toward the homies and locked eyes with Spider. He looked up really fast as if to ask if everything's cool, but all I could do is roll my eyes. Finally, Topper finished talking, I agreed without reading the fine print, and we headed back to the rest of the homies. A few minutes later, handball games were back in motion and the yard seemed to be back to the normal ticking time bomb. The Blacks could retaliate at any second. Spider and I excused ourselves and walked laps around the track. I noticed we had a few other homies in tow; kind of felt like our own security.

"So, talk to me dog, what that fool want now?" Spider asked.

"Topper gave me the keys to our cell block. I really didn't expect him to do any of this. As a matter of fact, I really didn't want any of it," I said.

I explained everything Topper had instructed. Spider's ears weren't missing a beat. He listened to everything without interrupting and just kept nodding his head. However, Spider convinced me otherwise. He saw it as an opportunity to make some money as gambling and drugs flowed through our hands and into the cell block. He also liked the respect that we were being shown by other inmates.

The next day I was excited to go to work. I wanted to find out about Ms. Sandoval. When I got there, I didn't have a job anymore. There was a White guy in my place. He said it was his first day. I looked over toward her office, but there was a new guy in her place. I approached him.

"Excuse me, C.O., I'm inmate Rocha, was wondering if I still have a job here?" I asked.

He stood up and grabbed a log board, looked it up and down, and sat back at his desk.

"Nope, no Rocha here, I don't have you on my roster," he said. There was a pause. I looked around the kitchen.

"By the way boss, do you know what happened to Ms. Sandoval, or if she's been moved?" I asked rather hesitantly.

I didn't know how this fool would react. He looked up at me.

"She quit last month."

The four words crushed me. The little bit of hope was not to be. I was more confused than ever. *Why did they crack my cell open this morning if I had no job?* I headed back to the yard. I took the long way and walked by the library. I wasn't ready to go inside yet, but just walking by gave me chills. Soon, thoughts of Ms. Sandoval became like vapors in the wind. There was nothing I could do anyway. I dove deeper into the prison politics abyss; successful in every aspect and lethal with every prison hit. I was becoming what I once feared.

I'm not going to lie, but once I settled in, I too liked the money that flowed in and the respect we got on the yard wasn't too bad either. So, there it was, Spider being my roll-dog, he pretty much took care of everything. We began making money and gaining more respect amongst the homies on the yard.

"Okay you're done," Big Dave said, as he started to dismantle the tattoo gun. "Keep it out of the sun." Walking away, I looked down and I could clearly see the fine detail of my Aztec culture tattooed on me. It had been 18 months since the FM incident, a lot more hits occurred since then, and my status kept elevating me to a higher echelon, but now things had changed.

A note was brought in from an inmate released from the SHU. It was addressed to me and me only. I didn't usually have this happen, but this was coming from a very powerful source—a head figure from Topper's crew. I took the note back to my cell and read it. I needed a witness, so I showed it to Chico and Spider. I walked back out to yard, gathered them, and we walked to the nearest table. I could see Topper and his crew at the far end of the yard. They looked like they were sleeping, but they were smacked back on heroine. "Here, I want you guys to read this, and rip it up after," I said, handing the note to them. "I'm going to take a piss, I'll be back." I walked toward the same outside restroom Spider flushed the knife in.

What they were reading was an order given to me to take out Topper. He'd stole more than the usual kick down and their drugs never made it to them. This was an ongoing issue, way before he got here, and now it fell on my lap. *Why me? Who the fuck knows?* The sun was setting and I wished more than anything that I could be home. I took a piss and washed my hands. I was stuck looking at FM's desk through the library window. I could see a vague image of FM writing, then his voice chimed in and I could hear his letter:

Dear Youngster.

I imagine you must find it a bit odd that I have written the words, "I forgive you". I did it for a couple of reasons. First of all I'm not exactly sure where I am headed. But, if somewhere there is a loving God, and if I am going to ask him for forgiveness for all the evil and sadness that I have created, I'd better be willing to forgive those who have trespassed over me. I thought you would be a good start to that. Secondly, I am old and tired. My body was never going to be able to leave this place. No cop-killer ever would. For years now I have been thinking that the only way to get out was to leave my body here.

When I had learned that Topper was in the prison, I knew that it had to be either him or me, but I have given up that fight long ago, Youngster. And I am okay with that.

And lastly Youngster, I had to forgive you because you are only a cog in wheel of a great machine that manufactures hate and evil by the truck loads in all kinds of shape and form. This motion has been put forth long before you got here and it will exist long after you are gone. You won't change it and couldn't change it if you tried.

You see youngster most people think we just lose our freedom because we are not able to walk the streets out there. But what we truly loose is the ability to make the choices we want in here. By virtue of our skin color we are unable to care for the ones we'd like to care about or associate with the ones we would like to associate with. And it is only if we are lucky and can thread a needle do we find someone, no matter what color they are, that we want and have the capability and ability to teach. You were a good student, Youngster.

For now do what you need to do to survive. Finish your time in here and get out. Never the victim. Enlist whoever you need to accomplish that as you have been enlisted to do other people's dirty work. Choose wisely.

By doing so, like you, he will become a powerful piece in the game. Never turn your back on him. Never take him for granted.

Walking back towards Spider, I smiled. I had made my decision.

"Look Fernando, I have a few homies that could handle this fool."

"No good," I said. "It has to come from somewhere else."

Just then, a voice came over the intercom yelled, "Escort. Escort." From a distance Spider, Chico, and I could see that a bunch

of newbie's entered the yard, and it was then that I saw him—someone who reminded me of myself.

"See that fourth guy in line over there?" I asked Spider.

"Yeah sure, the kid with the shaved head, tattoos on both arms?
Yeah, sure I see him," Spider said.

"Have him come over and see me."

With that last sentence uttered, I knew that I would probably
change this young guy's life path forever. If I had chosen right,
Topper would more than likely be hit by the end of the week.
Looking at it from the outside in, one could say that FM was getting
his retribution post-mortem through me. Last but not least, perhaps
I was increasing my chances of survival; to one day walk the streets
of Los Angeles, to be free, and the freedom to make better choices.
None of this could be certain. The only thing of assurance that I
held was this: that the cycle of prison would carry on. I would push
a gear to cause another gear to move and the evil of the California
State Correctional Facilities would stay intact.

I was about to choose someone, like those who had chosen me,
and those before them, and make him, "THE PAWN".

www.ingramcontent.com/pod-product-compliance
Lightning Source LLC
Chambersburg PA
CBHW050845180626
46814CB00007B/2637